THE GUIN SAGA

THE GUIN SAGA

Book Two: Warrior in the Wilderness

KAORU KURIMOTO

TRANSLATED BY ALEXANDER O. SMITH
WITH ELYE J. ALEXANDER

VERTICAL.

Published by Vertical, Inc., New York.

Originally published in Japanese as *Koya no Senshi* by Hayakawa Shobo, Tokyo, 1979.

ISBN 1-932234-52-7

Manufactured in the United States of America

First American Edition

Vertical, Inc.
257 Park Avenue South, 8th Floor
New York, NY 10010
www.vertical-inc.com

Then, as if drawn by an invisible thread, they followed the road to Nospherus. Above them the dawn star shone, guiding them to their proper selves.

—From the Book of Illon

CONTENTS

Chapter One

ACROSS THE RIVER OF DEATH

—— I ——

It was dawn in the Marches.

The morning mist formed a pale purple veil above the surface of the Kes. Across the river lay a no-man's-land, a rugged wilderness of rock and sand that stretched all the way to the horizon. The meager tufts of grass were the same color as the sand, possessing a kind of harsh beauty and pride that said, *Here is no cultivated soil, no verdant grove, no country path. Here is only death.* On maps these wildlands were shown as part of the Marches, but compared to the thick green woods on the side of the Kes where Rinda stood, they were another world entirely.

The leafy boughs of the Roodwood looked peaceful. *But looks can be deceiving*, thought Rinda as she stretched her arms to the sky and yawned. Half of the forest lay in ashes, and the Gohran stronghold that for years had towered in its midst was gone.

"And to think it seemed so big, so...solid." Shivering, Rinda hugged her shoulders with her long slender arms. She shook aside the platinum hair that fell down across her shoulders and got into her eyes and looked up at the smoldering pile of rubble that had once been the keep. Thin wisps of inky black smoke still rose from the ruins in places. The near-impregnable fortress had fallen to an army of the Nospherus Sem tribes in the space of a night and a day. Rinda's pale violet eyes flared and she shivered again, though her boy's leather jerkin was warm enough. *How many thousands died here?*

"Did you say something, Rinda?" came a sleepy voice from behind her. She turned to see her brother stepping up alongside her. The morning light shone down on them, illuminating a masterpiece of creation: beautiful, fine-featured faces that would have been nearly identical were it not for Rinda's longer hair.

Standing next to her, the boy looked like a highly polished reflection, peering back at her with the same exquisitely colored eyes. Only their expressions were different. Remus, prince and rightful heir to the throne of Parros, had the look of a dreamer. There was a softness to his stare and a gentleness in the way his lips parted, tasting the cool morning air. But his sister, the princess Rinda Farseer, had the hard, resolute look of someone who had seen too much at too young an age.

Right then, she was remembering. This was not the first time she had seen towers fall. The spires of the crystal city of Parros, too, had seemed impervious until the barbarous Gohran soldiers trampled the cobblestones of her home beneath their heavy boots. On that day in the War of the Black Dragon, when their father and mother, the king and queen, were put to the blade, Rinda and her brother had been saved by an ancient device hidden deep within the Crystal Palace. Yet a mistake had been made, an error in calculations, and they had found themselves transported out here to the Marches of

Gohra, only a short distance from the wildlands of Nospherus. The twins and their strange new traveling companion had been caught and taken prisoner at Stafolos Keep, and Rinda didn't know whether it was luck or fate that hordes of wildling Sem had attacked the Gohran keep that very night.

The warrior Guin had rescued them from the keep's burning roof. Now he was numb to the world, fast asleep behind a boulder at the base of the cliff that rose up from the Kes to the ruins of the keep. The Sem forces had finished their looting during the day and left the night after the attack; by the time that Guin declared it safe enough for them to emerge from their hiding spot, the chariot of the Sun God Ruah was shining again on the land. The tension of the long wait had melted away and they had slept.

Guin might have been in a sleep deeper than the dark pits of Doal, but Rinda knew that if there were even the slightest suspicious sound, he would be on his feet in a flash, wielding the longsword which even now lay ready across his knees. She smiled, and brushed her grimy locks back to fall over her shoulders.

"Rinda."

Remus had finally swept the last sleepy cobwebs out of his head, and now whispered to his sister in a low voice, as if he feared to break the morning's silence.

"We made it, didn't we? We're alive."

"Of course we're alive," she snapped back at him.

Remus blanched. "Not so loud, Rinda—what if they're still around somewhere…"

"They aren't!" the girl exclaimed, utterly sure of herself. "Even you should be able to figure that out! The Sem know that the smoke from yesterday's battle was like a giant beacon to the other Marches keeps. Why, reinforcements from Alvon and Talos will probably be arriving sometime today, I should think. The wildlings know that, and that's why they left in the night on those canoes—they were scared. Otherwise they would have spent all last night piling up the dead and having a victory feast. And that was good for us, too. If they hadn't been in such a hurry to get out of here, do you really think they would have left without searching for survivors?"

"I guess not."

"Really! I swear you only use half of your head most of the time." Rubbing her empty stomach, Rinda broke off her attack. She sighed. "Anyway, I'm really quite hungry. I'm sure there're fish even in these parts, but after seeing all that blood in the river yesterday, I'm not sure I fancy eating anything from the Kes. Did you see all those dead Gohrans and Sem get swept downstream? I'm sure this morning the fish have bellies full of them!"

"Ugh! That must be why it's so clear now. And to think that it was full of blood and corpses just last night," Remus murmured in genuine amazement.

Rinda clicked her tongue. "They were washed downstream, silly. No matter how many fish there are in there, they couldn't have eaten all that in one night!"

Rinda was wrong, but she had no way of knowing it. Being a young princess raised in the tranquility of the Middle Country with all the care given a delicate flower, the true nature of the river known as the "Black Flow" was a mystery to her, and she gave it no more thought. Right now she had more pressing concerns than the ecology of some wildlands river. "I really think I'll die of starvation…though that might be preferable to dying at the hands of the Gohran reinforcements. If we don't want to be found, we'd best move out of here…"

Rinda's voice trailed off as she looked around. She shook her head. The waters of the Kes offered little hope of safety, and turning back into the forest behind them would put them right in the path of any Gohran scouts. And who could know what barbarous and fiendish things might rampage through the wildlands that stretched as far as she could see on the other side of the river?

"I hope Guin wakes up soon and lets us know what he plans to do," Rinda muttered, chewing on her lip.

Remus tried his best to sound encouraging. "We'll be fine. I'm sure Guin will find a way to get us through this."

"Well, I hope so, because right now we've got a choice between the wildlands and the Roodwood, and that's no choice at all!" Rinda exclaimed; but her expression softened when she turned around.

"Suni…Guin!" she called to their two companions, who had finally emerged from their nighttime hiding spot behind the boulder and were walking towards her.

They made quite a couple. Suni, the young Sem girl, almost had to run to keep up with Guin's long strides. Rinda noted, too, a slight wariness in the way the child glanced from side to side as she moved. It was understandable, after the terror of the last two nights. Why, Rinda and Guin had saved her from a certain and grisly death no less than three times since they had met—once from her own kind! Suni was a Sem, but from the Raku tribe, a rather gentle clan compared to the violent Karoi Sem who had led the attack on Stafolos Keep.

There were other differences between the various Sem tribes, though most were about the same in appearance: around three feet tall, of slender build, with a bristly coat of fur covering their hands, their feet, and even their faces. They looked more like monkeys than humans, and conventional wisdom was that their capacity for rational thought, too, was more on the simian side. But they were not mere beasts, Rinda had learned that much.

They had a rather queer, complex-sounding language, and they could make weapons that pierced Gohran steel. They had demonstrated that they knew how to use fire, too, in the siege of the keep. They wore clothes of a sort: cut animal skins and crude cloth. Most of all, they could feel affection and love; one look at the devoted reverence in Suni's acorn eyes as she gazed up at Rinda made that clear.

In contrast, the leopard-headed warrior Guin revealed nothing in his expression. Like his identity and his past, Guin's face was a complete blank. Rinda found herself thinking back to when she and her brother first saw him: stripped of his memory and his possessions, wandering out of the darkness of the Roodwood.

He slowed to walk beside Suni, the morning sun glinting off

the tawny fur of his mask. He was more than twice the little girl's height, and at least six times her weight, though not an ounce of that incredible bulk was wasted. The muscles that ran like banded steel across his chest spoke of years of hard training. Had there been any doubt that here was a true warrior, the dried blood on his tanned skin and the innumerable battle scars— some old, some fresh—would have provided proof enough of the terrible conflicts he had withstood. And of course, topping his godlike form was the leopard mask, concealing his true features with those of a beast. He towered, a figure of violence incarnate.

"Are you rested up?" Guin asked in his low rumbling voice—a voice that the twins had only recently learned to understand without considerable effort. "You'll need your strength. We'll be in danger if we're not free of these Gohran lands by sundown."

"Leave Gohra?" said Remus, his eyes wide. "But how?"

"Simple. We need only to cross the river and we'll be in the wildlands...you know that much, do you not?"

Suni came up with a quick shuffle and threw herself at Rinda's feet, gazing longingly up at the princess's silvery hair. Rinda, absentmindedly patting the girl's head, was transfixed by Guin. He looked like something out of legend as he stood by the banks of the Kes bathed in the ruddy morning light.

"B-But if we go out into the wildlands..." Remus shivered and gulped.

"You know a better way? I thought long on this last night. We must cross the River Kes, somehow, then cut through the wildlands of Nospherus until we arrive on the eastern edge of the Middle Country. Any other route would be more difficult and more dangerous. Particularly as, with myself and Suni in the party, we cannot pass incognito through the human lands of Gohra."

"But the wildlands of Nospherus?"

"You're forgetting something, Guin! There is another way," came a voice from behind them. The four turned to see the ruggedly handsome and still youthful face of the Crimson Mercenary, Istavan of Valachia.

Two nights before, when Guin and the children had fled from the rampaging Sem and the Roodwood specter that haunted the halls of Stafolos in the guise of the keep-lord, they had been chased to the roof of the black tower. There, Guin was faced with a choice: perish at the hands of the pursuing hordes, or trust himself and the children to fate and the roiling black waters of the Kes far below. Rinda still remembered what it felt like as they leapt, she clinging to Guin's belt: the fear of flying through the night, then the jarring impact with the water's surface, then nothing but watery blackness swallowing the four of them whole.

Whether they were lucky, or whether Jarn Fateweaver was watching over them, she did not know. But they had lived. Jumping from a height of several hundred feet, they could easily have missed the deep water and struck the jagged boulders jutting out along the riverbank. Such a fall surely would have broken every bone in their bodies. As it happened, however, they had hit the river towards the middle, and after sucking them in it spat them back out to drift along with the current, unconscious from the impact.

Then luck favored them again. Floating defenseless in the Kes, it would not have been long before a large fish—or far worse—found them. But there had been someone hiding in the rocks at the base of the cliff, watching as they plummeted from the sky like a giant bird that had lost its wings. It was Istavan.

The young mercenary from the seaside region of Valachia, as cheerful as he was crafty, was congratulating himself on his escape from the cell next to that in which Guin and the boy Remus had been held. Anything was better than going to the block for a trivial bit of insurrection against the lord of Stafolos Keep. The beast-man and the boy could be damned for all he cared—Istavan made his own fate, and he was willing to get around anything in his way, even taking apart a wall brick by brick, which is exactly what he had done. He had climbed down a makeshift rope of torn bed sheets until he was below the walls of the keep. He had known he didn't have much time left, just as a torqrat knows when to escape a sinking ship. There was a reason he was known as "Spellsword": he had an almost supernatural nose for danger...and Stafolos Keep reeked of it.

His timing was perfect, too. Had he sat wasting in his cell any longer the Sem would have killed him along with the other captives in the tower; and had he escaped any earlier, he would have run headlong into the Sem armies as they came prowling up the shores of the Kes in the night. Then, no matter how great a warrior he was, he would have stood little chance against the endless battle waves of the tiny wildlings.

Jarn is fickle: for, had the guards on watch heard the sounds of a fight breaking out at the foot of the cliff below their walls, the fate of the entire keep would have been different that night. As fortune would have it, however, it was just after the Sem forces had quit the banks of the Kes to split into two strike forces, one in the heavy cover of the woods, the other along the cliff side where it wound away from the river, that Istavan lowered himself carefully down his knotted ladder.

The mercenary of Valachia was still in his hiding place at the cliff's foot when Guin and the children made their daring plunge. He sat where he was, watching their shapes bob up and down in the river for quite a while before coming to the conclusion that he would probably be better off with allies.

He crawled warily from his hideout. Finding a rope and grapple next to the remains of a boat on the bank, he tossed with a sure eye and, after a few tries, managed to hook the floating figures. With much effort he dragged them out of the water, and just in time, for as he finished pulling his waterlogged catch onto the rocky bank, the muscles in his arms knotting and bulging with the strain, a great wave broke the surface of the thick, dark, and deceptively quiet river water as a giant mouth rimmed with ferociously long teeth clamped down right where the four had been. The monster snapped its jaws two or three times more before finding the corpse of a keep guard floating nearby. Grabbing the dead man in its maw, it disappeared once more beneath the waves.

Istavan whooped, then made a sign to ward off demons. "A

bigmouth!"

After making sure the fiend was gone, Istavan examined his catch. And what a catch it was! He passed over the little Sem girl and turned all his attention to Guin. After shaking the unconscious warrior vigorously, he attempted to gently lift off the miraculously life-like leopard mask.

"By the flaming hackles of the hell-hound Garmr!" Istavan murmured in amazement, "this thing's really real—he's got the head of a leopard! And I thought he'd stuck on a mask in a fit of drink, or to hide his face from the guard." Whistling appreciatively, he knelt down to give Guin's muscles a prod, then drew the longsword from the scabbard at Guin's side. At last, his face deep in thought, he turned to where Rinda and Remus lay; and his long, slitted eyes suddenly narrowed. "This is that kid from the next room—and that must be the girl he was talking about. Aye! By the pallid face of Aeris, give this girl ten years and she'll be starting wars between the closest of friends, she will. This is no common peasant girl, I'd stake my sword on it. Now just you wait, Crimson Mercenary, this might be the start of something very profitable!"

Thereupon Istavan sat down, his legs crossed under him in the Valachian style, and stared at Rinda's beautiful, sleeping face as though he would never tire of it, excitedly muttering to himself—until suddenly he sprang to his feet with a grunt.

A lone Sem had come sneaking up on him from behind, either a straggler from one of the wildling armies or a rogue out to do mischief. Just as the mercenary noticed him, he let fly a poisoned arrow—but it flew too late. Istavan's blade flashed even as he twisted artfully out of the arrow's path, and the Sem's head flew through the air to land with a plop in the Kes.

The mercenary glared and spun around, checking to see if the little rascal had any friends waiting in the shadows. As he did he heard a rustle. Guin and the others were waking.

The four companions had spent the night hidden in a hollow among the boulders, in the care of the Crimson Mercenary.

"I couldn't help but overhear your conversation." Istavan folded his arms across his chest and favored Guin with an ironic sneer.

Though not quite of Guin's stature, Istavan was a very tall man. When it came to breadth, he lagged well behind the leopard-headed warrior. Istavan's body was slender, like a whip, but he was strong and agile—as those are who have lived the life of a mercenary from the age of twelve. He was wearing Gohran armor, minus the crests and insignia that his captors had torn from him when they threw him into the tower cell. At his belt hung two blades, a longsword and a shortsword, and his boots were of ankle-high leather.

He wore his helm with his faceplace set back, letting the sunshine fall on his youthful features. He was around twenty, with a tight face and a shrewd look in his eyes. *A long face*, thought Rinda, *but not unattractive*. His black hair was cut short in the Mongauli fashion, and a sarcastic smile stretched between his taut, almost sunken cheeks.

Yet perhaps the most striking thing about the mercenary were the black eyes that sparkled and shone out of his tanned face. They were always scheming—even the way they blinked was somehow crafty. But they had a certain charm, and they were so vibrantly full of life that the unwary might find themselves smitten with this man from Valachia even if they knew they couldn't trust him.

"There is another way—is that what you said?" Guin asked, turning his expressionless leopard head to face the soldier.

Istavan nodded impatiently, straining to understand Guin's muffled voice. "We all made it through the other night one way or the other, and, to our great fortune, the Sem decided to pack up and leave. But, like you say, if we wait around here we'll be found by Gohran troops sooner or later. So we leave. But first there's something I need to do."

"What?"

"Eat." Istavan grinned and reached behind his back and, as if by magic, brought out bundles of food: cold meat and grain balls that he had taken with him when he escaped from the tower.

Just seeing food made the twins drool. Istavan generously doled out his stash to everyone, though his face took on a grudging expression when he gave Suni her portion.

Together, they all sat down to break their fast. Sitting atop a flat boulder, they pushed the pieces of meat into the grain balls and ate as they talked about what to do next. Suni aside, they all shared the same goal: to somehow cut across the Marches and return to civilization, all the while avoiding Gohran territory.

As Istavan said, "The Sem girl has friends out here, I'm sure...and I'm done in Gohra—nobody will hire a wanted man.

Truth be told, I was in a bit of trouble back in the capital—that's why I joined the Marches patrol in the first place."

Istavan's face lengthened into a sour grin.

"I...er...shortened the life of a kid back in Torus, turned out to be the son of a noble. They put out a warrant for me in Yulania, so I made my way down to Kumn...where I got into a bit of a duel with someone...that's when I came back out to Mongaul. Yep, I don't have a shore to sleep on in any of the three duchies of Gohra. And I've pretty much had it with these monkeys out here. That leaves Cheironia way up in the north, or the ancient Kingdom of Hainam..."

"Well, we..." Rinda began, but then she thought twice about saying too much. It was clear that Guin still didn't trust this Istavan. "We were planning on going to Cheironia ourselves, or to Earlgos."

"The Earlgos grasslands, eh? Wasn't the king of Parros's—rather, I should say the *late* king of Parros's younger sister wed into the royalty out there?" Istavan asked. His tone was innocent, but he watched the twins' startled reaction closely. They glanced at each other, but did not answer.

"What about you, leopard-head?" Istavan prompted.

"I..." Guin paused, thinking. "I must find out what the word 'Aurra' means. If I find that out, I might discover who I am, and how I came to be like this. That is all."

"So, there's no objection to going through the Marches in the direction of Cheironia, then."

"None."

"Then it's decided!" said Istavan cheerily. "Now, as I was

saying before—about the other way we could travel—if we're lucky, we might just find one or two rafts back in the keep that weren't destroyed in the fires. Hell, even a damaged one will do if we can repair it. The way I see it, we could get on one of those and just ride the Kes River out of this place."

"Ride the Kes?!" shouted Remus, startled. "Are you crazy? No one's ever gone down the Black Flow and survived the trip— even I know that! We learned it in our classes! The Kes is the border between civilization and the *wildlands*, the lands of Nospherus! They say there're horrible things in there…things not from our world."

"Boy, I knew that and more about the Kes before you were born! I was making my living on the battlefield while you were still in dirty diapers." Istavan laughed out loud, ignoring Remus's fierce glare.

"Even so—why go down the Kes?" asked Rinda, thinking that her brother was quite right to be perturbed.

Istavan flashed the pretty girl a mischievous look. "The Kes reaches the sea at Rosmouth. In the town of Ros, we can find a merchant ship to take us across the Lentsea. From there, it's an easy matter to go to Cheironia or even Valachia if we want, and then we're free to do as we please."

"Though I doubt any merchant ship would take me on as passenger or crew without suspicion," Guin observed.

Istavan guffawed, licking the grease from the cold meat off his fingers. He let his laugh rumble on for a while before he spoke again. "Yes, we do have to do something about that big leopard head of yours." The mercenary's voice was serious, but a derisive laugh still sparkled in his eyes.

"If there were anything he could do about it, he would have done it a long time ago," Rinda said protectively. "I think he's under some kind of curse—otherwise he should be able to take the mask off. Maybe if he hid it with a hood or something..."

"He'd stand out all the more that way." Istavan waved his hand in the air dismissively and took a swig from the canteen at his belt. "We can worry about that once we reach a town. The bigmouths and the other carrion feeders in the Kes couldn't care if he was a leopard-headed freak or a full-blooded beast. Both taste the same, I'd wager. Still..."

Istavan gave Guin a long look-over, then whistled. "You have to wonder what chain of events led what wizard to use his powers to make something like you! I've fought on battle-grounds all over the world, from Queensland and Taluuan in the north to the archipelagos of the south, from beautiful Simhara to the mudlands of Lute; I've even gone all the way to god-forsaken Ferah-la, Kingdom of the Cripples, and I've seen more and heard more than I care to remember...but I've never heard of anything like *you*....

"Little girl, you probably don't know about the Ice Queen Tavia who rules the frigid snows of Queensland? She's trapped in ice, and yet she lives! Then there was the ruler of Simhara, jewel of Corsea. He was half-man, half-bull, a great priest...with a tail! But it turns out his bull head was just a mask, set with gems. Aye, that was right freakish, but like a good half of the strangeness in this world, it was the result of man's mischief.

"But anyhow—this leopard noggin is something else!"

Istavan stared at Guin and sighed. "It's like someone ripped the head off a warrior and slapped on the head of a real live leopard from the grasslands of Mos, but kept the warrior's brain in there somehow, and his soul…maybe. Gaa…it's enough to drive a man to mulsum, just looking at it. I don't like things without good logical explanations, see."

He acts as though it were his problem, thought Rinda angrily. *It's not as if Guin chose to become like this!*

"You're right, little girl," said Istavan calmly. Rinda jumped—she was sure she hadn't said anything, but Istavan answered her thoughts as if he had heard. "He was turned into this leopard-headed monstrosity by someone else, and through no fault of his own. That's why it makes sense he wants to find this 'Aurra'—it could be the key to finding out who he really is! I'd do the same if I were in his shoes.

"Still, there's just something odd about the situation, leaves a sour taste in my mouth, and I swear I won't get a good night's sleep until I get to the bottom of it. Don't you see? It's like some thing is behind all this, pulling the strings; and the Crimson Mercenary, Istavan Spellsword, is not going to sit idly by! You shouldn't either.

"I mean, it's like the—hey, little girl, have you heard of the Shining Lady?"

"The Shining Lady?" Rinda thought for a moment. She could swear she'd heard that phrase somewhere before. She and Remus exchanged glances, then she shook her head. But when she asked Istavan to explain, he only mumbled something, then fell silent. She asked again, but Istavan ignored her and rose abruptly, brushing bits of grain off his knees with his hand.

"Now's no time for small talk! Well, what'll it be? Do we follow my plan of finding a raft and going down the Kes to Rosmouth, or do we not? Do you want to wander forever in the pathless wastes of Nospherus, fighting barbarians and fiends and worse...or do you want to ride the Kes? Sure, we might have to take care of a few nasties along the way, but once we reach the sea, it's smooth sailing to Cheironia. I'll have to go find us a raft. Reinforcements from Alvon Keep are bound to be here soon, and we'd better be somewhere other than here when they come—so make up your minds quick."

The twins held hands and looked nervously at each other, then at Guin. Suni couldn't understand what they were saying, but she could sense that they were talking about things of great importance, so she sat quietly in the shadow of the boulder, chewing what was left of her food. Istavan's jet black, impatient eyes sparkled as he watched the twins, waiting for them to make a decision.

Guin's expressionless leopard head slowly nodded, an unfathomable expression in his yellow eyes. Slowly, his mouth opened. Even Istavan understood that whatever Guin said now would determine their course of action. Somewhere along the line, without so much as a word, it had been decided that Guin was their leader. Surely, this had always been the case no matter where he went, or with whom he traveled. The proud princess of Parros, too, waited for him to speak; for this accursed, leopard-headed warrior had an aura of majesty about him—the kind of aura that surrounds one who is destined to rule.

In his thick, gravelly voice, Guin spoke—

"If we're looking for a raft, we better start in the under-ground cellars."

Istavan slapped his knees. His armor caught the sunlight and shone black like his obsidian eyes. Their path was decided.

—— 2 ——

Finding a raft wasn't as difficult as they had expected. The Sem had been thorough in their siege, but they weren't the least bit interested in the Mongauli boats and river gear stored in the underground cellars.

In their looting, the raiders had chiefly sought out the high-quality Gohran crossbows, pausing occasionally to pick up scraps of Gohran cloth to make into clothing. Plants that bore enough fiber for weaving were scarce in the wildlands, so the Sem had adopted the custom of skinning the few wildlands animals they could kill, or on occasion, members of enemy tribes, and tanning their hides to wear. Now Rinda and Remus tried to ignore the naked corpses that lay strewn about the ruins of the once proud keep. The gruesome sight of the carnage disturbed Suni so much that she clung to Rinda's shirtsleeve and only let go after much coaxing.

The ghastly scene seemed to have little effect on Guin and the mercenary Istavan. They mechanically tossed aside the corpses to make a path, stopping to clear a number of the fallen from before a pair of great, charred doors. Istavan looked almost slender beside Guin's powerful frame, but his thin arms were amazingly strong, and he picked up the heavy armor-clad bodies with ease.

When the doorway was cleared Istavan advanced through it to investigate. A short while later, he gave a shout. He had found a raft in the cellars, untouched and in perfect condition.

The craft was quite sturdily built. It was made of hard planks of wood bound together tightly with bands of iron, and though it was shallow, it had something of a hold where provisions could be stored. There was also a mast, which would allow them to run up a sail. A broad, flat raft was better suited than a regular boat for riding the Kes. The river's banks were far apart enough to accommodate its width, and the swift current would easily capsize a narrower vessel.

All five of the companions—even little Suni—were drenched with sweat by the time they finished dragging the raft out to the courtyard. Then Istavan directed them to gather up thick branches to use as rollers, and, pushing and pulling, they slowly made their way to the outer wall.

There they wondered how they were going to get the raft down the sheer cliff to the river, but a simple solution presented itself. Istavan went back into the keep and returned with a rope and pulley that the keep guards had used for lowering rafts to the water. They took turns on the pulley, and after a good deal of sweaty work, the raft was on the riverbank. By now the sun had risen high into the sky and was blazing down mercilessly.

They had to rest. The sweat poured down their faces and stung their eyes. Even the thought of the approaching Gohran reinforcements couldn't stir them to move. The heat and the effort had left the twins of Parros exhausted; Rinda was barely aware of Suni fanning her with a giant leaf. Even Istavan was covered with sweat, his shoulders heaving with every breath.

"You sure you're human, leopard-head?" grumbled Istavan.

If Guin was tired, he didn't look it. His chest was barely moving.

"As sure as Cetoh the serpent munches on his own tail, if you're human, then I don't know what we are! You've the strength of an ox!"

Guin didn't bother to reply.

The mercenary looked over at the raft it had taken them so long to get down to the water. His thoughts were still racing. "Aye, she's a beauty, isn't she? Built tough for crossing the Kes. Still—hey, Guin, you know what they had us mercenaries do when we first arrived? For months we were down here, trying to join rafts in a line across this blasted river—trying to make a bridge for that crazy duke. See, Archduke Vlad, he wasn't happy having anyone, even a river, tell him where his borders lay, and here his northeastern edge runs along the Kes. So he says build a bridge, raise a big army and make the wildlands of Nospherus Gohran territory! Trying to get a leg up on the other two arch-dukes, I bet. Tario of Kumn and Olu Khan in Yulania might be interested to know of his plans. Aye, Vlad wants land so bad he's making eyes at Nospherus!"

"This is none of my concern," replied Guin, matter-of-factly. He had no way of knowing that he was wrong—not in his wildest dreams would he suspect that, in the not too distant future, the insatiable hunger of the Mongauli archduke would matter very much to him, and that his path would be forever determined as a result.

Istavan looked at the twins who lay exhausted near the cliff edge where they had fastened the pulley. "We better bring as much food as we can find, and water. The water of Kes is no good for drinking, and I've no intention of eating anything that's been swimming in there. And...weapons." Istavan sounded as though he'd given similar orders many times before.

The specter of the Gohran reinforcements rose again in their minds, and the twins and Suni got up and scampered about the ruins, bringing back what food they could get their hands on, though that was neither plentiful nor very appetizing. Most everything edible had been seized by the Sem, and what jugs of water and wine were not taken had been smashed.

Still, they found some dried meat and fruit, and some flour that could be mixed with water and eaten. This they divided up and placed in leather satchels that they hung from their belts. Istavan joined them, occasionally stooping down to search the bodies of fallen Sem.

When Rinda asked him what he was looking for, he flashed her a shameless grin. "Just looking for shiny trinkets they might have stolen, you know?"

Rinda frowned. This man was even more unscrupulous than she had thought! She would have to keep an eye on him.

Then, as though he could read her thoughts, Istavan turned around. "Hey, little girl, why is it you want to go to Cheironia, anyway? Where are your parents? You're no peasant girl from around these parts, that's for sure."

Rinda flinched, then retorted, "I could ask you the same! And who's the Shining Lady, anyway? You're looking for her, aren't you?"

Istavan laughed heartily. "You've got spirit, girl. I'd hate to have you as a daughter! Think of the trouble!" But he sounded more bemused than critical, and there was a twinkle in his eye. "You know, with the sunlight shining on your hair like that, you look like a pretty doll made out of silver. Maybe you're the Shining Lady I'm looking for, eh?" He laughed again. "What house are you from, girl?"

Why, of all the insolent, nosey... Rinda was growing more aggravated by the moment, and she bit down on her little ruby-red lip to stop herself from giving him the tongue-lashing he deserved. Remus, looking concerned, came over to see what the matter was. Rinda silenced him with a look and shot back at Istavan, "Our family and past are no concern of yours. Even if I were the one of whom you speak, I daresay I'd have nothing to do with the likes of you!" Rinda brushed the platinum blonde hair he had just complimented back over her shoulders.

"Ah, but if you *were* the Shining Lady, you *would* have something to do with me, for she is the keeper of my fate."

"The...keeper of your fate?"

"Yes, though truth be told, I'm not really sure what that means. A fortune-teller—"

Istavan's mouth snapped shut, as though he had suddenly realized he'd said too much. Rinda was going to try to coax more out of him, but at that moment Guin returned with Suni at his side. He carried a crossbow in each hand and looked about warily as they approached.

"We leave now," the leopard warrior announced, without so much as a greeting. "There's smoke rising in the direction of the Taloswood. If I'm not mistaken, those are the lunch fires of the troops from Alvon or maybe Talos. It's only two and half days on horseback down the main road between Stafolos and Alvon. That means that scouts riding ahead of the main group should already be in the Roodwood by now."

"The journey is quicker by river—we'll be past Alvon by nightfall. Let's get moving," Istavan urged, heading for the cliff. Remus, Suni, and Rinda rushed to follow him along the narrow track winding down the cliff face to the river.

The companions' chatting was replaced by cautious silence. They moved like hunted animals. Guin peered back at Stafolos Keep hoping that no trace of their presence remained, before turning to follow the others down. Nothing lived in the gutted ruins. The purifying flames had burned away everything, even the evil, corpse-eating spirit that had cursed the place and its master. Guin muttered in approval.

When the leopard-man jumped onto the raft, the iron-bound logs rocked under his massive weight. Istavan slid over to the far side to balance the load.

"Girl-child, get closer to the mercenary. Suni, stay in the middle—yes, right there."

Guin got the other passengers into position as Istavan

shouted "We're off!" and swung his sword at the rope mooring the raft to a boulder at the water's edge, cutting it cleanly. His voice had a boyish ring to it, as though he were remembering his childhood in sea-faring Valachia. No sooner had he cut the rope than the swift current swept the raft and its five passengers away from the shore, carrying them out towards the middle of the great black flow of the Kes.

Rinda shivered and grabbed on tightly with both hands to one of the iron rails that ran the length of each side of the raft. The river was flowing fast, indeed!

"Listen up!" shouted Istavan over the roar, "Don't any of you fall in, 'cause at this speed we'll be long gone before we miss you!"

Guin braced his legs at the stern and pushed off the river bottom with a long pole, keeping them on a straight course.

The sun was blazing hot, but a strong wind blew on the surface of the river, sending up a fine spray of water that soon cooled them almost to a chill.

Shortly, Rinda began to get used to the speed of the raft. "What beautiful water!" She leaned over the side, looking down into the eddies as they rushed past. "Why, I think I can see rocks on the bottom! It's hard to believe that anyone would call this the Black Flow."

Istavan quietly shrugged and shook his head. He was sitting on one knee at the front of the raft, his left hand gripping the rail and his right holding his drawn sword.

"Look closer before you speak," growled Guin. "The river is far too deep here to see the bottom, and from where I stand looks black as death. If you say you saw rocks, we'd best be care-ful—the creatures of the Kes wear many disguises.

"Don't forget where we are, children! These are the Marches, and nothing is safe."

The leopard-man never ceased making minute adjustments to their course as he talked, working the long pole through the water behind them.

Rinda and Remus looked at each other, their eyes wide; then both nodded.

"I'm sorry Guin...but look at how far away Stafolos is now! At this rate, we'll be at the river mouth in no time at all!"

Istavan called back in a calm voice. "From here to the town of Ros is a good thousand tads—many days on horseback even if you could go straight along the river. The current may be fast, but surely we're not moving much more swiftly than that...which means we're spending more than a few days at the mercy of this river of death. Best pray that Jarn's watchful—and in a good mood!"

"I only spoke my thoughts," said Rinda grumpily. Her plat-inum hair flew back, sparkling, in the wind off the river. Istavan gave a shrug and grinned.

All of them turned their full attention to keeping the raft on course. Yet even if they had not been so preoccupied, it is unlikely that any of them, even Guin with his sharp eyes, would have noticed the figure on horseback high above them atop the Gohran cliffs on the starboard bank.

It was a knight, steed reined to a standstill, who stared down at the Kes far below. The knight's faceplate was down and from atop the well-wrought helm a white tassel fluttered beautifully in the breeze. The knight's armor, too, was white, with white gauntlets and greaves. Even the horse wore barding of white leather, set with sparkling gemstones.

The knight's eyes studied the river from within the white helm. From the height of the cliff top, Guin and the others on the raft looked like little ants clinging to a leaf.

The strange knight watched them for a short while as they fought bravely against the current and their uncertain fates, then gave a satisfied nod and pulled the reins to turn the horse away. Long, shiny blond hair spilled from beneath the white helm.

"Hyah!"

The rider urged the horse on with a crack from a small riding crop held in a silvery-white chainmail glove. The white horse stepped lightly away from the cliff and disappeared down a narrow path—a shortcut through the forest that led to the keep at Alvon.

Quiet returned to the Marches woods and, down on the Kes River below, the five raft riders were unaware that they had been observed.

Remus shouted through the white water-spray from the side of the vessel where he was holding tightly onto the rail. "Hey, Guin—say we get to Rosmouth okay—how are we going to hide your head? And what about Suni—"

"A way will present itself."

"But Suni—"

"We will drop her off and she can return to her own people."

"Ach, you're like a girl," Istavan sneered. "Always worrying about this that and the other thing. Your sister's more of a man than you, I'd say."

"Hey, that's not—" began Remus, always sensitive about being compared to his sister—but he never finished his retort. Instead, his face went white, and his grip tightened on the rail.

"What's wrong?" Rinda demanded.

Remus responded in a shaky voice, pointing out into the river. "L-Look, over there! Something's odd!"

"Odd?" Rinda shot him a doubtful look, then glanced across the water and gasped. "What *is* that?!"

A great swell of bubbling whitewater was rising up only five yards away to their right and rapidly approaching, chasing the raft—

Then the frothy water split, revealing a creature that seemed to be made entirely of long rows of bone-white teeth!

"Bigmouth!" shouted Istavan, shifting his grip on his sword.

The enormous jaws opened, and came straight for them.

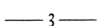

—— 3 ——

Rinda's scream shot out across the water. In shock she let go of the rail and covered her face with her hands.

"Fool!" Guin reprimanded her even as he thrust the pole vigorously through the water behind them. "Never let go of the rail! Grab on with both hands or you'll be knocked over!"

"And I'd say that thing's mouth is big enough for you!" Istavan added in a shout. The mercenary was himself holding the rail with one hand, his sword gripped firmly in the other. His eyes were fixed on the creature coming towards them through the water at full speed.

And what a creature it was! Rinda didn't have to look twice to see why it was called a "bigmouth." Indeed, the thing was only that: a giant, living mouth! When it opened wide its maw it was nearly two yards across, broad enough to swallow either of the twins whole. And the teeth! Row upon row of sharp daggers gleamed like those in the murderous jaws of a Lentsea shark.

Yet even more disturbing than the maw itself was the lack of anything behind it. For where there should have been a body—a head, fins, a tail—there was absolutely nothing. The whole of the bigmouth seemed to be those snapping, slavering jaws. It was a minion of Doal come into the world to sate a bottomless appetite for destruction.

Rinda trembled, her mouth gaping as she stared at the nightmarish monstrosity. The mouth shook almost as if in a rage as it bore down upon them. Every time it snapped its jaws shut, water jetted out in its wake in a spray of white foam. This was how it moved, Rinda realized. By spurting out water behind itself in one direction, it virtually ate its way through the river in the other!

Worse yet, every time the creature gulped, the waves it created rocked the raft violently, forcing those aboard to grip the rails with desperation as their foothold tilted precariously under them.

"Guin! No!" Rinda's scream could barely be heard over the crash of a sudden wave that surged across the deck, sweeping Guin's feet out from under him. He had been wielding the raft-pole with both hands, relying only on his preternatural sense of balance to keep his footing.

Luckily, the waves had pushed the small craft closer to the east bank of the river, where the channel was not so deep. Though his feet were in the air, Guin found the rocky bottom with his pole, and thrusting it downwards he used it as a pole-vaulter would, sending his massive body back through the air with surprising grace. He landed squarely on the raft again, still carrying the pole that was their only means of piloting their vessel.

"Guin!" Remus's cry of relief was choked with tears.

"It's coming!" The Crimson Mercenary shouted out in

warning. "Hold on tight, and flatten yourselves to the deck! If you don't want to die, you'll keep your heads down. I'll slice that Doal-spawned thing in half if it's the last thing I do!"

The creature lunged!

The jaws snapped, sending water spraying in all directions. The monster's hunger was almost palpable; clearly its intent was to knock its prey off the sturdy raft into the water, where it could feed at its leisure.

"Look out!" Istavan shouted and swung his blade through the air. But the wave of water that the creature sent before it smashed into him with full force. He did not drop his sword, but he was forced to lunge for the rail and hold on for dear life lest he be swept over the side.

Rinda's screams rose above the rushing waves. She had pressed herself to the deck, hanging on to the rail as she had been instructed, but when the disgusting monstrosity snapped its jaws right above her head, she looked up—and saw there, peering out from within its gaping maw, a small pair of eyes that looked straight at her, shining with primal hatred. Rinda had had the best tutors in all fields, but never had she heard of a beast that kept all of its sensory organs inside its mouth!

Its strange body structure only made the monster's attacks all the more viciously accurate. As the bigmouth flew up out of the water, over the heads of Istavan and the twins, it twisted in mid-air. Trailing a stream of water, it lunged straight for the warrior Guin, who was still manning the pole at the stern.

The creature's chosen prey did not stand there waiting to be eaten. Guin swung the long raft-pole up into the air, and as the bigmouth descended on him, he swiftly thrust the pole into its jaws. The jagged teeth began to snap together—and Guin swung the pole wide.

Propelled by Guin's leverage, the bigmouth was thrown to one side. It hit the water with a loud smack and disappeared beneath the surface…but the suction caused by the great thing pulled on the raft, and the deck lurched precariously toward where the bigmouth had gone down.

"Hiiii!"

"Suni!"

The jolt shook the little Sem girl's numbed hands loose from the rail and she staggered and began to topple over. At that moment the familiar swell of white water signaling the bigmouth's return reappeared just a few yards away and began to race back toward them. Suni was falling into its path.

Rinda screamed. "Somebody save her!"

Guin's long arm darted out over the water, plucking the little girl out of the air in the nick of time, lifting her back onto the relative safety of the raft. The bigmouth veered and kept its distance for a moment, spraying froth over the river behind it, as though it was considering another attack…but then it sank under the waters as suddenly as it had appeared, fading quickly into the depths.

For a while, all on the raft were silent.

"Phew!" Istavan broke the quiet with a sigh of relief, like someone waking from a bad dream. "What a beastie that was! By the white nipples of Istar, and the thousand fangs of Garmr! Hey, anybody get eaten?"

No one laughed at Istavan's jest. He turned and began wringing water from the sleeve of his tunic. "To look at us you'd think we were caught in a squall at sea!"

The five companions were drenched with river water from head to toe. They spent the next few minutes wringing the black flow from their clothes and spreading out what garments they could upon the deck.

Rinda edged over toward Suni, who clung trembling to the railing. "It's okay, Suni. It's gone, now." She patted the tiny girl's shoulder. "We're safe. Safe."

Guin alone seemed unshaken. He stood astern, quietly plying the single oar-pole in the water behind them, steering them away from the rocks that lined the wildlands bank of the river, pushing them back towards the middle of the flow. His yellow eyes flashed, scanning the water, checking to see that no bubbles rose.

"It seems to be gone," he said at last. "It must not have been too hungry. And it was small for a Kes bigmouth. We were lucky." Guin shook his leopard head to dry it like an animal would, the spray of water forming a halo around him.

"What? You mean there are more of those things out there? And bigger?!" gasped Remus.

Istavan chuckled. "Plenty of 'em, boy! And there's worse than bigmouths in the Kes. How else do you think the river got so clear and clean this morning, when it was filled to overflowing with the bodies of the dead just yesterday, eh? The foul creatures of the Kes are always hungry."

"It seems that we have been spared on account of those

corpses," noted Guin.

"Indeed!" Istavan smiled at the leopard-man, then looked down at himself and moaned. "Argh…I'm wet down to my skivvies—and my dry rations look like soup!"

To the twins, it felt as if the attack had gone on for hours, but in reality not even a *twist*—one turn on the small sand clock— had passed during the whole ordeal. The Kes had again taken on its peaceful veneer, and the blaze of the sun reflecting off its smooth surface quickly dried their drenched gear.

"Do you think it will be back?" Remus worried.

"Of course!" replied Istavan cheerily. "But don't worry—in my half year of soldiering in this forsaken place, I've handled more than my share of bigmouths and giant leeches."

But it was Guin that drove the monster off, thought Rinda. *This mercenary of Valachia has a bigger mouth than anything living in the river!*

The Crimson Mercenary shot a glance at Rinda, his black eyes sparkling mischievously. He looked almost as if he were about to retort to her unspoken criticism, but instead he curled his upper lip into a sneer and said nothing.

The raft continued swiftly down the river, the single pole guiding it through the now smooth waters.

The rider came galloping through the gates of Alvon Keep, his swift horse lathered in sweat. Count Ricard, keep-lord and commander of the Fifth Red Knights, was waiting in the court-yard for the report. He had sent messengers out along the highroads that spread like a spider's legs from the capital of Torus, and this was the first to return.

The count's face turned white. "What's this? Already in the Alvonwood, you say? Why were there no signals from the towers? But no matter, now—bring my horse! I will at least ride to the gates to give welcome—"

"There will be no need for that, Count Ricard," came a crisp voice from above and behind the flustered lord. "I am already here."

"Wh-What—?" The count turned and looked up at the wide, crenellated wall that ran around the inner courtyard.

There, atop the wall, was a mounted warrior with a white crested helm and long white cape, astride a pure white steed fitted with white harness and barding—the same rider that had spied on Guin and the others from the high Gohran cliffs above the Kes.

The warrior lightly spurred the horse and descended the stone steps into the courtyard, rider and mount moving as one. Several other knights, all garbed in white, followed by the same route. From a distance they appeared similar enough that any of them could have been the leader; but from nearer at hand it was clear that these others' fittings and armor were far more simply decorated than were those of the speaker.

"To travel with such a small retinue, really—" Count Ricard began, but the leading knight, who was now dismounting with the help of three retainers, dismissed his remark with a wave.

"A detachment of my white knights waits in the Alvonwood. Send for them, and provide quarters here that they may rest. And...do not ask me yet why I have come here."

The rider's voice was clear—a young, crisp voice that

inspired in the listener a desire to view the face of its owner. There was something noble in it, too, a charismatic power—the natural ability to command that is reserved for the highborn.

The count, though he was no commoner, and was moreover slightly taller than the leader of the white knights, bowed deeply in greeting.

"It shall all be as you command."

"Stafolos Keep has fallen," said the knight matter-of-factly. "Alvon is now the vanguard of the Marches defense."

Ricard—the hardened veteran of a hundred battles—bit his lip and swallowed. "I sent a squadron of cavalry to aid Count Vanon as soon as our watchmen spotted the black smoke. I had thought they would be arriving at the keep by and by—"

"They were too late. The Sem tribes have not crossed the Kes in such numbers since the moss year—doubtless even Vanon had grown unwatchful. Thus Mongaul has lost Stafolos Keep. It is a step backwards in our plans for Gohra."

"We should have been more diligent in our communications, General," Count Ricard said, standing up to his full height and pulling off the sword at his waist, scabbard and all, to hold it to his left breast in the Gohran salute. The knight-general reached out with a white-gloved hand and placed the sword back at Ricard's waist.

"You are not at fault, Count." The charismatic voice was bracing. "Stafolos is lost, but rather than ask why it fell, we would do better to think about what we must do next. You have heard of the…complications with the Black Dragon War?"

"Yes."

"Then you know that, after years of planning, a grand force of our elite units launched a surprise attack on Parros, jewel of the Middle Country. Yet while the Crystal Palace fell to our hands, and the Priest-King Aldross the Third, and his wife, Queen Tanya, are no more, some members of the royal family evaded capture by our black knights…"

"The princess Rinda and the heir to the throne, Prince Remus—the 'Pearls of Parros,' correct?"

"Indeed. We know not what crafty white magic they used, but we received reports soon after that they had been spotted in the Roodwood. Believe me, the Golden Scorpion Palace is burning with curiosity as to just how two defenseless children could not only evade our elite warriors, but then travel from the heart of the Middle Country all the way to the Marches of Rood in a single night!

"If there is something there we do not know of, some secret principle of the workings of our world we have yet to grasp, then the answer to this mystery could very well be the key to commanding not only the three realms of Gohra, but the Marches and the whole of the Middle Country as well!

"Now—Count Ricard."

"Yes, General?"

"Do you not see a connection between the twins' appearance in the Roodwood, and the subsequent fall of Stafolos Keep?"

"A connection?" Count Ricard swallowed nervously. "Do you ask me in your station as the archduke's representative, General of the Right, captain of the white knights?"

"I do."

"Then…as much as it pains me to admit it, I can think of no way in which a small boy and girl could have taken any part in the destruction of a place such as Stafolos Keep, with its ten full squads of knights and their infantry support!"

The general's voice cracked like a horsewhip. "Fool! It was the army of Sem that destroyed Stafolos, that much is clear." Count Ricard blanched.

"What I am asking you is whether or not you find it strange that the children and the Sem should have appeared at the same time. Is it impossible that the orphans of Parros and the Sem tribes of Nospherus are in league?"

"But that is madness!" The count in his surprise let the words spill from his mouth. "The most ancient of priestly lines of the Middle Country consorting with monkey-men from the no-man's-land?"

"Do not be so quick to disregard the possibility, Count," the general replied, pointing the horsewhip out over the keep walls in the general direction of the Kes. "There is a chance, infinitesimal as it may seem, that Parros has managed to join forces with the barbarians of Nospherus. Were they to gather what loyal soldiers survived the Black Dragon War and together launch an attack to avenge the crystal city, Gohra would be faced with an assault from the rear! We must move to make sure this does not happen, no matter how scant the possibility. And Count, there is something else you should know.

"I rode here along the cliffs that look down upon the Kes…and there I saw the strangest thing."

"One of the foul river creatures, perhaps? They are common enough in these—"

"No," the general cut him off, "What I saw was most unusual—a lone raft bearing down the Kes, probably from Stafolos, rushing past Alvon, perhaps destined to go all the way to Rosmouth via Tauride."

"A lone raft on the Kes?" sputtered the count, breaking out into laughter. But then, a thought silenced him. He had heard rumors that this rider in white, the right hand of Archduke Vlad himself, was a stern punisher of failure with a particular dislike for carelessness. He had best not seem impudent before this one. The count cleared his throat and looked serious.

"The Sem, perhaps?"

"No," the general replied after some thought. "Though I cannot say for sure *what* it was. My eyes can see a falcon many tads distant, yet I still have doubts about what I saw on that raft.... There were five people aboard: two men, and two women—perhaps they were children—and one smaller passenger that looked much like one of the Sem. And one of the men..."

The count leaned forward, his curiosity piqued. What could possibly be so unusual as to give the infamous General of the Right, mouth of the Archduke, pause?

"One of the men...he seemed...*strange*..."

"Strange, you say?"

The general chuckled dismissively. "No, it was probably a trick of the light. Yet it seemed to me that the larger of the men on the raft had the body of a warrior from the neck down, but the head of some great cat—a leopard or tiger!"

"A leopard?" Now the count had to steel his jaw to keep from breaking out in laughter. Surely the light had played a trick on the general's eyes! But Ricard had an idea what sort of reaction the general expected of him, so he quickly offered to send riders in search of the raft.

"No need. I doubted my eyes myself, and so, before entering Alvon, I sent word by the fires for a small squad of my own white knights to go down to the river to find out just who is on that raft...and bring them back to me, if need be."

The count was impressed. Here was someone who let nothing pass by and who knew how to get things done. But he had no time to linger on his thoughts, for the general spoke again.

"Prepare a troop and two squads of knights—we may need them to fish that raft out of the Kes. I assume that the river-crossing exercises, which were discussed at the palace assembly at the beginning of the tea moon, have been proceeding according to plan?"

"Yes, General."

"Very well. Then have those squads prepare for a river crossing, should the need arise. And should any word come from the signal fires about Stafolos Keep, do not delay in sending this response..."

What the general said then was enough to shock the count into asking a rather more pointed question than he would normally have dared to pose to one who so greatly outranked him: *What had led those assembled at the Gold Scorpion Palace to make such a decision?*

"No questions will be necessary," came the reply he should have anticipated. "All you need do is to ensure that my orders are carried out swiftly and to the letter. I have come along the road from Torus with little rest and less sleep. I am weary. Prepare chambers for me—I will sleep until the signal comes."

"As you command."

The count sent a page running to prepare the chambers. Meanwhile, the general slowly began releasing the straps on the great, ornamented white helm.

Count Ricard stood silently watching. He was not ignorant of what the general looked like, yet it was always a sight worth seeing, and so he waited.

The general's slender hands finished untying the last strap and pushed the white-plumed helm backwards. At once a radiant glow spilled forth from the figure that now had the attention of all in the courtyard.

At first it seemed as if the knight were lit up with some inner brightness, but in fact the glimmer was no more than sunlight falling upon locks of golden hair. Count Ricard almost gasped despite himself, enchanted by the image before him. Here was true beauty! The face that the helm had lifted to reveal was that of a young woman, her features so splendid that surely they were unmatched by any save those of Irana, goddess of battle and the hunt.

Studied closely, her face seemed more that of a girl than of a young woman. But already her presence projected a commanding aura of dignity. Her form was framed by her flowing golden hair, which tumbled halfway down her back, and her lips were set with such a look of determination that the count felt certain nothing would ever break her will. But what joy it would be to receive a smile from those lips, so pink and full! And her green eyes, as deep as the River Kes, were filled with a resolve and passion rare even in the most extraordinary of men. She was noble, yet shining with ambition; cool, yet elegant and gracious.

The young general was truly a study in beauty. Though not fully mature, she held all the promise of dawn on a beautiful and holy day. *No*, thought the count, *hers is not the pallid and willowy beauty of Aeris, but that of she who stands ever armored with vine-wrapped spear next to her beloved husband, Ruah, sun of the land—she is the war goddess Irana come in white armor!* It took the count a moment to realize that the sigh he heard was his own.

Just then, the page returned.

"Your chambers are ready, Lady Amnelis."

She nodded and made her way through the courtyard. By now there were none in the keep who did not know that the archduke's famed daughter Amnelis, captain of the white knights and commander of the lightning force that conquered Parros, was at Alvon.

—— 4 ——

Meanwhile, back on the raft, several *twists* had passed without any unwelcome visits from bigmouths or giant leeches or any of the other horrors of which Istavan warned. Once again Rinda was beginning to find their trip down the ever-widening river quite pleasant, much to her surprise. The golden chariot of Ruah had raced swiftly across the arch of the sky and was now slowly dipping down toward the mountains. It was easy to forget that this was the Marches and that the river that bore them onward was the black Kes.

The deep green of the Marches forest extended without a break on their starboard side, the unchanging scenery interrupted only once by smoke rising from the cooking fire of a borderland homesteader.

Occasionally, though, there were creatures to be seen. A long-tailed bird with feathers of ruby red and coal black took flight from the treetops, its piercing screech trailing behind it. A tan water snake flexed and sped across the surface of the water, wriggling out of the path of the swiftly moving raft.

To the port side stretched the ash grays and light browns of the Nospherus wildlands, a barren vista of rock and sand. There were some signs of life in the wastes; here and there faint green lichen clung to the rocks. Yet the bleak expanse was a far cry from the lush green of the opposite bank and only served to confirm what the settlers said: that Nospherus was a no-man's-land, where only barbarians and evil creatures dwelt.

Far beyond the sands, the gray, jagged silhouette of a mountain range rose like a distant mirage. "The Ashgarn Mountains, ceiling of the world. They stand between the Marches and the Northlands." Istavan pointed toward the far-off range. "Queensland, ruled by a queen who lives forever in the ice, is beyond those peaks. Somewhere up north too is Taluuan, home of the giants. Then there's Vanheim, land of the gods, ruled by the hero Bardor; and beyond that, Norn, the northernmost land in the world, or so they say."

The others did not speak. Undeterred by the lack of response, the Crimson Mercenary continued his impromptu lecture.

"The thing that used to get us mercenaries wondering the most is why in the world, with all the perfectly good land to be had, Gohra or the Mongauli archduke was interested in *this* forsaken waste of a place? Aye, we spent many a night after river-crossing practice in hot debate over just that question. The Gohran Marches may not be my idea of paradise, but you can make a living there, and it's green, by the gods! But cross this hell-river and you're in no-man's-land. Jarn was in a peculiar mood indeed when he put these two side by side.

"Or maybe he knew what he was doing, laying the river here to keep the men on their side and the fiends on the other.

Though he had some help from the bards in that. The stories they told of poisonous vapors, death to breathe, kept most folk out of Nospherus for the longest time.

"And those weren't the worst of the tales! They say the two races who do live in Nospherus, the giant Lagon and the tiny Sem—neither of which you'd call human—were once just like us, but as they lingered under the spell of the wildlands their forms gradually changed and their minds became barbaric! My grandfather's a kitara player of some fame back in Valachia, and as he tells it, there's a foul mist, a humor in the air, that changes the creatures that live in the no-man's-land. It makes them unnatural, monstrous. That's why you get things like the bigmouth here in this river, and on land, the sand leech, the flying velolith, and mouth-of-the-desert—not to mention the fiendish creations of Doal that don't even have names!"

Istavan suddenly turned to Guin. "Say, leopard-head, maybe you came from around these parts?"

"Guin's no fiend!" shouted Remus.

Rinda shot a cold glare at the brazenfaced mercenary. Guin merely shook his tawny spotted head as if to say he did not know.

"You should have remembered something by now, even a little. I have to wonder: are you as brainless as a Kes river snake, or do you just want us to *think* you are, eh?"

"Istavan! You shameless…idiot!" shouted Rinda furiously.

The Crimson Mercenary laughed a gravelly laugh. "When you lose your temper, the violet of your eyes deepens to purple, like two evening stars in the twilight! Why don't you turn those stars to the water and watch for that bigmouth, eh? We'd best be ready next time it comes."

"Scum!" hissed Rinda loudly, but in spite of herself she turned furtively to check the water around them. Twilight had come upon them. They were near Alvon now; before long they would be coming to Tauride, the northeastern corner of Mongaul.

They ate a simple meal of dried meat, dried fruit, and a few vasya that they had collected when they were provisioning the raft. A few *twists* in the afternoon sun atop the raft had dried out their clothes, so drenched just a while ago from the fight with the bigmouth, so that it seemed they had never been wet at all. Guin continued to wield the pole, tirelessly keeping them on course.

"It's too quiet." Istavan spoke between bites of vasya fruit.

"I rather like the quiet," Rinda responded, glaring at him. There was something about the mercenary that made her irritable and anxious at the same time. Why did he always seem to be up to no good, and why was he always grinning like that?

"I said it's *too* quiet. I find it hard to believe that the Kes, hell's river itself, is just going to let us float on down like lovers on a summer sail…no, something's going to come, and we'll be lucky if it's only twice the size of that bigmouth."

"Is that what you *sense*, Istavan 'Spellsword'?" the princess teased. She had heard enough of this scoundrel's empty boasting to last her a while.

"You might say that—hey, leopard-head, you aren't planning on us spending the night out on the river now, are you?"

"Of course not," came Guin's reply from the stern. "The

black river is no place to be after nightfall, unless you're fiend or demon. Staying out here would be suicide. We'll pull up to shore just before dark, make a campfire small enough to avoid detection, and take turns on watch. We can resume our river journey in the morning."

"Good idea!" Remus sounded rather more relieved than he had intended. Rinda only just managed to keep from shouting an exclamation of relief herself. She was glad they had Guin, a real warrior, protecting them. To think how it might have been if they had been stranded out here with only the so-called Crimson Mercenary...they would have been appetizers for some fiend three times over by now! Istavan himself seemed to accept Guin's leadership of their little party, though Rinda did not like one bit the way his eyes always seemed to be laughing at them, plotting something at which she could only guess. The girl shivered.

"My thoughts exactly," said Istavan, seeming not to notice the twins glaring at him. "Things will get easier once we're out of Mongaul. After Tauride down to the city of Ros, the river runs along free settlers' land."

"Yes," Guin agreed, "but tonight we will have to risk sleeping on the Mongauli shore. Spending the night in Nospherus would hardly be better than spending it here on this raft."

Istavan grunted his approval, quietly staring at Guin. In the course of their short journey so far, Guin had often noticed the Crimson Mercenary's eyes on him, perhaps more frequently than could be attributed to mere curiosity about his leopard head—though Guin could not think of any other reason for

Istavan's interest.

Guin raised his face, his wild, yellow stare meeting the unwavering gaze of those black, laughing eyes.

It was Istavan that turned away first, on the pretext of looking up at the cliffs on the Mongauli bank. He squinted, and suddenly grew serious.

"Guin!"

The mercenary did not yell, but hissed in a low, tense voice. The leopard-man had just begun steering the raft in toward the bank. The water was now painted red by the setting sun.

"Someone's there!"

"What are you talking—" began Remus, but Rinda grabbed his arm, cutting him off. Istavan squinted at the woods upon which the dusk of twilight was slowly falling, searching for movement. Then he waved back at Guin.

"Wait, wait, keep us in the deep—I'm sure I sensed...there! On the bank, where the woods come down to the river. There are more than a few of them!"

"Gohran soldiers!" gasped Rinda.

Istavan glanced at her out of the corner of his eye. "Maybe— or maybe Jarn is in a generous mood and it's only some local homesteaders—but wait! By the white steed of Irana!"

"There's a squad's worth, maybe more," Guin calmly noted.

"What's this? Those are no regular troops, they wear white!" Istavan's distinctive features twisted into a grimace as he leaned out over the railing to get a better look at the riders. He could now clearly see a squad of white knights spilling out of the

50

deepening shade of the forest on the far bank.

Though it struck fear into her heart, Rinda found that the scene had an odd, dreamlike beauty. The riders came drifting out from under the trees like white ghosts, then spread sure-footedly along the riverbank. All were attired in pure white, as though they had been cut from the ice that capped the Ashgarn peaks. White cloaks fluttered behind them, and simple white plumes fell back gracefully from their helms. Their horses, too, were all white, each one fitted with the same white barding.

"They wear Gohran armor," Guin observed.

"But—white knights? That's impossible!" Istavan groaned.

"Why not?" Rinda said. "Everyone in the Middle Country knows about the five knightly orders of Mongaul, the black, the white, the blue, the red, and the yel—"

"Save your lecture," said Istavan, brusquely interrupting her. "Little girls shouldn't speak of things they know nothing about. Stafolos was guarded by the count Vanon's Third Black Knights; Alvon is defended by the Fifth Red under the banner of Count Ricard. The black and the red guard the Marches, you see?"

"And the white—?"

"Are led by Lady Amnelis, daughter of Archduke Vlad himself, and General of the Right. They are the archduke's guard, stationed in Torus, which is why not one, certainly not a whole squad, should be out here in the boondocks."

"But there they are," said Guin.

Istavan's only response was to irritably rap his hands on the railing and turn back to watching the knights. Then he frowned. Their luck, it seemed, was turning for the worse.

What little hope Guin and the others might have had that the riders had not noticed them was shattered when the largest of the white knights moved his mount to the edge of the river and cupped his hands around his mouth.

"You there, on the raft!"

Guin and Istavan quickly exchanged glances. The mercenary slowly reached for the sword at his waist, but Guin shook his head firmly. They were only two, and the knights were a full squad; furthermore, it was not clear that they meant Guin and the others any harm.

"Well?" said Istavan in a low voice that sounded like the purring of a cat. "We've not much time until nightfall!"

"Let them make the first move," was Guin's reply.

On the bank, the white knight called out again, louder this time, as if in doubt that they had heard him. "You on the raft! We are the Marches patrol, from Alvon Keep. What are your names, and where do you go? Stop your raft on the bank and speak with us!" He waved one arm toward a low part of the bank that could serve as a landing.

Istavan clicked his tongue. "Me and the twins might be able to talk our way through this, but leopard-head and the monkey girl...hey, Guin, I think a quick escape's our best bet."

"No," said Guin slowly. "Look."

The others on the raft looked at the knights and groaned in unison. It was clear that the Gohran warriors, whatever their purpose, had no intent of letting the raft pass them by. Even as the captain called out to the companions in a reassuring voice, the other knights, following quiet orders, had spread out in a fan formation behind him. Now a full thirty crossbows were pointed at the raft, ready to fire a hail of stone shot should the adventurers not comply.

"What business is it of yours what we do? We are travelers! Why do you trouble us?" yelled Istavan angrily.

The white-garbed captain swung his horsewhip in a commanding gesture. "I'll ask the questions. I've strict orders to bring all on that raft to Alvon Keep. Now come ashore, or be shot: the choice is yours."

"Great," grumbled Istavan. "Guin, let's skedaddle. Children, lie flat on the deck. They won't be able to hit us with those crossbows once the sun goes down."

"Hold on tight," said Guin in an even voice, and pushed off with the oar-pole on the river bottom, giving the raft an abrupt burst of speed. The knight on the bank shouted for them to stop. Guin's pole found a sturdy rock and he pushed off again hard, sending them through the water so vigorously that a wave came spilling over the side. Then suddenly the air was rent by a terrified scream.

"Yipes!" Istavan whirled to see the source of the cry. It was Suni, clinging miserably to the railing, staring with wide eyes at...

"A bigmouth!" yelled Istavan, though by now all on the raft and the bank could see the great white swelling of water racing towards the raft at an incredible speed.

The rushing sound of water nearly drowned out the shouts of warning from the knights and the screams of the children.

Istavan cursed the accuracy of his prediction—the nightmarish monstrosity bearing down on them was at least three times as big as the last one.

"It'll break the raft!" he shouted, raising his sword to cut the great maw in half, and dropping to his knees to get better balance on the deck as it swayed and tilted violently in the spray of water from the fast-approaching monster.

A fearsome arc of enormous teeth, the creature lunged and slammed into the raft again and again, trying to knock Guin and the others off into the water. Each time it hit, the five clinging to the railings were tossed about like insects on a leaf in a rainstorm. Fighting back was out of the question; it was all they could do to just hang on for dear life.

Back on the shore, the knights, who had been ordered to capture the people on the raft alive, were frantically firing their crossbows at the creature in the river. But the few shots that hit did little to stop the thrashing monstrosity, and they were forced to shoot wide to avoid hitting the companions.

Even the agile Guin and Istavan Spellsword had their hands full staying on the raft as wave after wave rocked the raft. The bigmouth then slipped under the raft and smashed upwards with tremendous force. It was sure to capsize them soon, and then all would be easy prey for its blind, ravenous hunger.

Guin growled. The time to act was now! Letting go the pole, he slid across the deck, moving along the railing as the raft bucked wildly with every impact. With one hand still on the rail he drew out the shortsword at his waist—in the water, it would prove far more effective a weapon than his great longsword.

Quickly clenching the weapon in his teeth, he stripped off his baldric and threw it down on the deck to rid himself of its bulk. Only then did Rinda, gripping the railing near the bow of the raft with numbed hands, notice what Guin was doing and see the fierce determination of a wild beast burning in his yellow eyes.

The color drained from Rinda's face. "No, Guin! What are you doing?" She immediately began crawling down the swaying deck toward him. "You can't go! It will kill you!"

Guin took the sword from his mouth for an instant. "Hands on the rail, girl!" he roared, and clamped the blade in his teeth once more.

Just as he crouched, ready to spring into the water that now roiled from the bigmouth's violent motions like the pools of hell, Rinda screamed again.

"Wait, Guin—look! Something's happening to the bigmouth!"

All on the raft looked, and gasped.

The bigmouth was moving off to the side of the raft, and it looked as if the water around it had turned to a translucent jelly. No, it was something else: some creature had swum—if you could call its oozing motions "swimming"—right over the bigmouth, and was wrapping itself around the Doalspawn's bony mass.

"A swalloworm!" shouted Istavan, hope rising in his voice.

The massive, translucent creature's gelatinous body was covered with thousands of tentacle-like cilia. It looked like a gigantic lugworm, thought Rinda, at least three times as long as

Guin was tall. Searching for food to wrap itself around, it moved through the water by rippling its cilia.

Once it had established its death-grip, no amount of struggling would shake the swalloworm off. The thousands of cilia would then drag the prey into the monster's body, where it would be slowly and slimily digested.

So the bigmouth isn't king of the river, thought Rinda.

The bigmouth was panicking; it thrashed against its foe so violently that it made the attacks on the raft seem mere sport by comparison. The rays of the setting sun made the water red, and it looked as if the raft floated on a river of blood except where the surface was churned to spray by the struggling bigmouth.

No matter how much it tried, however, the great-jawed creature could not break free from the squiggling gelatinous grasp of the swalloworm. The hunter was now the hunted. Seized by a primal drive for survival, the bigmouth turned on its assailant and bit into the gelatinous body wherever it could. But the swalloworm did not bleed, nor did it seem to feel any pain, and its grip only tightened.

"Now's our chance to escape!" yelled Istavan.

"No good—I lost the pole!" shouted Guin.

Then he howled and Rinda screamed. The bigmouth and the swalloworm had twisted in a sudden fierce convulsion, creating a giant wave that flipped the raft clear over. The companions' hands finally slipped from the rail as they all fell screaming into the water.

"Everyone make it?"

Istavan was the first to pop his head back up out of the river, spluttering and coughing. His youth spent in the sea in Valachia had made him an excellent swimmer. Spouting a geyser of river water from his mouth, the mercenary started to make for the far Mongauli bank; but the sight of the knights pointing and shouting on the shore made him turn around. He didn't particularly want to stay out in the middle with the two monstrous beasts having at it, so with powerful strokes, he struck out towards the Nospherus side of the river.

Rinda had been fortunate. When the raft capsized, she had been thrown through the air to land in the shallows not forty feet from the Nospherus bank. And Istavan found her floating there. Grabbing her around the neck, he tugged her with him, stroking the water with one arm. it did not take them long to reach the bank. The Crimson Mercenary crawled up onto the rocks like a drenched torqrat and heaved the unconscious princess of Parros up behind him.

When Guin's leopard head broke the surface, he made the same decision as Istavan and began making for the Nospherus bank. Before climbing out onto the rocks himself, he threw little Suni up out of the river, then went to help the waterlogged Prince Remus pull himself out of the water. Istavan reached out a hand to the leopard-man, who scrambled onto the shore none too soon as the mass of living gelatin had made quick work of the bigmouth and was now streaking through the water towards Guin, its cilia rippling.

Up on the safety of the rocks, no one spoke for a long while. Their breathing was ragged, and they were once again soaked to the bone. Exhausted, they lay sprawled, glad to be feeling solid ground under them.

The sun had dipped below the horizon. The white knights on the far shore seemed a world away. *The far shore*, thought Rinda, who had come to and was coughing up the last of the water that she had swallowed.

For they were in Nospherus.

Chapter Two

THE BARBARIAN WILDERNESS

—— I ——

"You let them get away?"

The general did not raise her voice, yet its menacing tone was enough to make the hardened warrior blanch. Even the Gohran soldiers who stood nearby, red knights in stiff postures of attention under Count Ricard's watchful eye, shifted nervously in their armor. The Hall of the Lion was filled with tension.

The target of the general's wrath was an ugly giant of a man who stood with his white-plumed helm held to his breast. He was Vlon, one of the captains in Amnelis's personal guard. "Please, your forgiveness, General! We were—"

"Your excuses will not be necessary!" Her voice, now shrill, silenced the trembling hulk of a man. "I do not blame you for failing to capture them. We are all at the mercy of fortune.

"What I despise is your negligent decision not to follow them across the Kes, simply because you had received no such orders. You were aware of my desire to learn more of the strange company on that raft. Once you had found them, Vlon, it should have been clear to you that they were worth crossing the river to capture! Furthermore, you should have then sent a messenger to Alvon to report on the situation and to request reinforcements. I had Ricard prepare a troop and two squads, ready with rafts. They could have made the crossing quickly and captured the fugitives! Or perhaps you thought a crossing too risky?"

"Yes, General."

Vlon broke out in a cold sweat. He was a nobleman himself, from a family of long lineage in Torus with ties to Archduke Vlad. Yet there was none in Mongaul who would wish to parry words with the leader of the white knights, let alone cross her— after a manner, not even her father the archduke.

Amnelis had removed her white riding armor. In its place she now wore a long white robe that bared one shoulder, like a man's toga. Beneath that she wore a pair of slender trousers. Her magnificent hair hung loose to her waist, shining with a brilliance purer than Alceisian gold. She was truly a beauty, but curiously, her beauty was one that nudged the beholder to think of her as a handsome prince rather than a fair lady.

Her mouth was small, her lips shaped like the petals of a flower opening beneath the aquamarine glimmer of her cold, mysterious eyes. The combination of that gaze and her crystalline voice was more than most men could withstand.

It was too much for Vlon. His scarred face twisted in a grimace, and his head drooped.

Amnelis looked at him a short while longer, then spoke more kindly. "Very well. I trust that you will no longer simply follow orders like an automaton and will take advantage of such opportunities as are presented to you in the future. Perhaps

Count Ricard's men are crossing the Kes as we speak. Let us hope that I worry for naught." Amnelis turned away from her charge. "Count Ricard, attend me in my chambers, and bring the diviner Gajus with you."

"Yes, my Lady," said the count immediately, bowing deeply. He stood to watch the archduke's daughter walk away, her white robes fluttering behind her exquisitely elegant form—the slender, yet ruthlessly effective, body of a warrior.

He waited until she had left, then turned to the disconsolate giant.

"Bad luck, eh, Vlon?"

They were comparable in rank. Though Ricard, keep-lord of Alvon, commanded more men, Vlon was a white knight and a captain in the guard unit under Amnelis's direct control. Like Ricard, Vlon was a count of Mongaul, and the two had been friends for many years.

"Indeed, I did not know the truth of what the lady suspected. I only realized when I heard the report your knights sent back from Stafolos. Had I known the orphans of Parros were among that strange lot on the raft, I would have crossed the river on horseback."

"You did not know, and thus you are without blame," said Ricard, relieved in his heart of hearts that the blame was not on him.

"I was always with the lady-general during the Parros campaign! I was also with her when we withdrew early, for her protection. She did not have any more information than I did. Yet what we see in that information is as different as night and day, it would seem."

"And that is why she is a general, and the representative of the archduke, and you are not."

"Aye, old friend. Though she has lived not half the years I have, she sees things a hundredfold more clearly." Count Vlon sighed, then continued meditatively. "Ah well, that is past now...but what a strange country Parros is! It was an ancient land indeed, but that hardly explains the royal twins' trick of traveling across the whole of the Middle Country in a night. And when I saw that leopard-man, I doubted my own eyes."

"Surely, it is a mask of some sort."

"I did not think so, for it seemed the leopard fur grew most naturally out of the skin of his neck and shoulders. Nor would most masks I have seen stay on after such a violent toss in the water."

"I would not be surprised to find that the leopard-man is another reason for Amnelis's keen interest in that raft," said Ricard thoughtfully.

He could not have guessed the truth behind the destruction at Stafolos: that an evil spirit masquerading as the Black Count of Mongaul had been capturing Sem from the wildlands of Nospherus and murdering them, thus provoking the attack that destroyed the keep. Yet he had just heard the report from the signal fires that the fragmentary records that had been salvaged from the ruins of Stafolos included an astounding revelation. On the night of the attack, a strange, leopard-headed man and the twins of Parros had both been among the prisoners at the fortress—a fact that Count Vanon (in truth the spirit who ruled in his place) had neglected to report immediately. Since they were seen on the Kes, it seemed that the three had, by some miracle, cheated death in the blaze at the keep. And now it seemed they had escaped Mongaul altogether.

"I heard nothing in the crystal city about a half-beast in the service of the royal family. Something looking like that would surely have set people talking in every tavern in Parros! Where could it have come from?" Vlon wondered aloud.

Ricard shook his head. "I have no idea—I've not even seen this creature.... My friend, I beg your leave. It would not do for me to keep the lady waiting."

Vlon continued, seeming not to have heard him. "Parros was a cultured place, but militarily, it was no match for Gohra. The capital city was beautiful—like a dream. When the crystal tower fell...I felt our victory was almost too easy. It is strange. Even though the royal family is no more, and their kingdom only a memory, there is something of Parros that lingers on in my thoughts...."

A page approached and reported to Count Ricard that Gajus Runecaster had already gone up to the lady's chambers. Ricard hurriedly excused himself, but Vlon was too lost in thought to notice his friend's departure.

When Count Ricard arrived at the ample, if somewhat stark, chambers he had appointed for the lady-general, Amnelis was already deep in discussion with the caster Gajus.

In the center of the room sat a wide, coal-black table set with goblets and a large platter piled with fruits. The wiry, needle-thin caster had not touched even a drop of his water. The lady-general sat next to him, the hem of her robe tucked back so her slender trousers could be seen beneath. In her milk-white hand she held a silver goblet from which she sipped honey mulsum between questions, as if to help her clear her thoughts.

She turned to the count, speaking as soon as he had closed the door behind him. "Count Ricard, if we are to keep the minimum necessary number of men at Stafolos to help with rebuilding and defense, and a full guard at Alvon, how many men does that leave free for other duties?" Ricard knew better than to waste time on formalities. He replied immediately without ceremony.

"I have three battalions under my command, as you know. If the squadron I sent to Stafolos were to remain there, and a full battalion to guard Alvon, I have at your disposal, my Lady, two troops of knights, three platoons of footmen, and a transport corps with supplies."

"Gajus!" The general turned once more to the diviner. "Which will serve us better: to use what troops can be spared from the keeps of nearby Tauride and Gairun, with reinforcements later, or to send to Torus for a battalion of red knights?"

The diviner rubbed his skeletal hands together and croaked in a raspy voice. "Borrow troops from Tauride and send to Torus for reinforcements."

"But that will take too long," Amnelis replied, the words lingering on her lips. Ricard could practically hear her mind churning. It was all he could do to resist the urge to risk seeming impetuous and ask what she was thinking.

"Very well," she said with some finality. "Ricard, extra supplies will not be needed, but I must ask you for one more troop of knights. As for footmen a single platoon should suffice...on second thought, no. The ground in Nospherus breathes poison—lethal to anyone not mounted. Prepare three troops of knights for a river crossing. I will lead them myself—"

"Into the no-man's-land, my Lady?" Ricard burst out in shock.

"You had some other place in mind?" A faint smile touched the general's lips.

"That will not do! You must not go! As the loyal servant of His Excellency the Archduke, I cannot allow you to—"

"There is no time, Count Ricard," said Amnelis, reaching out a slender hand towards Gajus's crystal divination sphere. "I will not expose myself needlessly to danger, but should the path I must walk be fraught with it, I have no choice but to press on.

"Still," she said after a pause, "there is no need to go without taking necessary precautions. As I was about to say, your troops will build a temporary bridge across the river, and later a simple fortification to hold it on the far side, as we have been planning for some time now. The three troops I will lead once they have crossed into Nospherus. The unpredictable nature of the Kes has prevented us so far from making anything more permanent, but the bridge need only hold until reinforcements from Tauride and the expedition forces from Torus arrive. Then we can begin the main invasion of Nospherus."

"I-Invasion?" stammered Ricard loudly. Ever since the river-crossing exercises had been ordered he had suspected that the Golden Scorpion Palace had its eyes on Nospherus for some reason, but never had he expected a full invasion. What could they possibly see in that noxious, accursed land?

"The Golden Scorpion Palace takes the fall of Stafolos Keep quite seriously," Amnelis explained. "The border that runs from Stafolos to Alvon and on is not only a line of defense for Gohra; it is also the northwestern edge of the Marches. Stafolos was the key outpost of the Marches defense. Our greatest fear was that the remnants of those loyal to Parros might somehow join forces with the barbarian tribes of Nospherus and attack Gohra from her rear...a fear that has grown with the escape of the Parros orphans.

"It is vital that we hunt them down and question them before they join with the Sem. Even if our fears were groundless and the Parros-Sem alliance an imaginary threat, it would not do for us to sit idly by. Stafolos has fallen and there must be retribution! It falls to us now to campaign against Nospherus, and to destroy the main tribes of the Sem. You understand, Count Ricard, that especially now, when we have stretched our arms far into the Middle Country, we cannot suffer the depredations of our enemies here in our own backyard. Know also that the Mongauli attack on Parros was entirely my father's doing. He did it, of course, for the greater glory of the three archduchies of Gohra, and so Tario of Kumn and Olu Khan of Yulania have praised him well for that. But Mongaul's expansion has upset the balance of power between the archduchies. It has, shall we say, *strained* our relations with our neighbors. It is not unthinkable that Kumn and Yulania might join forces to put Mongaul in its place, should they feel the need."

"For Mongaul!" shouted Ricard, spontaneously leaping to his feet and drawing his sword. It was the Gohran salute.

"Yes...so you see why we—why *Mongaul*—needs Nospherus." Amnelis's eyes shone with an emerald light in the dim room.

"As...a bastion to protect our backs?" ventured Ricard, hesitant to put what he was thinking into words.

The lady-general, sitting there in her men's robe and trousers, gave a deep, throaty laugh.

"Yes, that is one reason."

"So, you mean to say that Mongaul will go to war with—"

"Count Ricard, this is a matter of the highest secrecy. Even in the Golden Scorpion Palace only a few are entrusted with full knowledge of our plans," Amnelis's voice was quiet but stern. She looked at Ricard directly. "Let me just say this. The no-man's-land of Nospherus is of vital importance, and we must move quickly before anyone outside of the Golden Scorpion Palace realizes this as well.

"Gajus!"

"My Lady?" answered the diviner in a hoarse croak.

"What say the stars?"

"Ah, I was just gazing at them while you spoke."

The aged caster set his divining board and divining sphere side by side, as if to compare what they told him, and rubbed their surfaces with his spidery fingers. "Not good...not good at all, what the stars say. Their positions are most peculiar."

Amnelis sat poised and still, waiting intently for his prediction.

Gajus groped at the diviner's cords around his neck.
"Frankly speaking, I do not clearly understand their message.
Yet I know something is beginning to move, to take shape—
something quite extraordinary.... Something, perhaps, that
shall sway events in the Middle Country for a long time to come.
The stars of battle and providence, and the pole star that sits on
the northern throne all pull against each other—soon they will
enter the same house!"

"What does that mean, Gajus?"

"It is a foreboding of change—of chance meetings and sudden decisions—of destiny in turmoil, my Lady."

Amnelis fixed the caster with a stony glare. When she saw
that he had nothing further to add, she lightly shrugged her
shoulders and turned to Count Ricard.

"You see, my dear keep-lord, diviners are all the same.
They appear to know, but then they do not, and nothing they
say is ever of practical value."

"The stars do not predict the future, Lady Amnelis,"
croaked the diviner, "They are merely a mirror, reflecting what
happens in our world. It is men who make things happen, and
fate—the threads of fate are many and tangled. We walk from
one to the next and even the greatest prophet cannot tell with
certainty where they lead."

"Yes, yes, I know all that." Amnelis waved her hand dismissively. "What you're telling me is that you don't see any omens,
good or bad?"

"I do not—which is to say that the struggle of the stars I see is
not one that bodes good or ill, nor are their final positions

clear—but it seems to me that the fate of many shall change…yes, it shall come like an avalanche, and soon."

"What about the leopard-man? I must know what he is!"

Ricard raised an eyebrow. "With all due respect, his peculiar appearance is probably the result of scarring from some illness, or perhaps a well-crafted mask…."

The count's words trailed off into the silence of the room. He remembered what Vlon had said down in the hall, and it occurred to him that Amnelis might not care to hear his opinion in any case. After all, he had not actually seen this half-man.

Amnelis did not honor him with a response, but instead turned back to Gajus.

"Well, Runecaster? Can you explain it? The world is wide, and the Marches are deep and full of strange monstrosities. Is there any record of a half-man such as the one I have seen?"

Gajus rapped the divining board with his long fingers and pondered. "I have delved into many mysteries during my years as a caster, but most of these were but aspects of man's everyday life, approached with the skills of my ancient craft so that they may be seen with new insight. But this creature you speak of is from an entirely different realm altogether: the realm of myth, not sorcery."

"Myth…Ah, was there not a myth regarding such a half-beast god? Cirenos, yes…" Amnelis reached out an ivory-white hand, took her goblet, drained it, and slowly stood. The folds of her robes swirled around her slender figure. "Regardless, if we capture them, part of the mystery will be solved. Indeed, we may find out all there is to know about this leopard-man."

"May I ask why my Lady shows so much interest in this creature?" asked Gajus abruptly.

Amnelis stopped and turned back to face him, seeming
almost startled.

"My Lady senses something, does she not? I said the stars
are gathering toward one house—it is the house of the Lion, and
the Lion is not unlike a leopard. It lies waiting in the very center, a great carnivorous beast. They are moving towards it,
changing their paths. And...my Lady, daughter of the archduke: of the many stars that now approach the Lion, there is
also the one that shone most brightly over the Golden Scorpion
Palace on the eve of your birth."

The caster appeared to have fallen into a trance now, his
eyes half-closed. The white edges of his eyes beneath his heavy
lids shone startlingly bright against the weathered tan of his face.
For a moment it seemed to Ricard as if the old man were listening to some sound from far away, but strain as he might, the
count could hear nothing. The deep hood Gajus wore cast his
face in a shadow, making his bony visage look like a skull with
jaws agape, trying to say something but lacking a tongue with
which to form the words.

Amnelis stood a moment, saying nothing. Her green eyes
shone with something that was neither shock nor rage nor
embarrassment, yet was all of these things at once. Her lower lip
moved as though she wished to respond, but was unsure of what
to say. Ricard held his breath.

Then, to the count's great surprise, the general's face broke
into a warm smile.

"Really, these things you say, Gajus! I think you have become addled by your years of staring into that silly ball!" Amnelis laughed heartily, then with a light rustling of her robes, she exited to make preparations for her expedition.

Left by themselves, the two men glanced at each other, and quickly turned away—Count Ricard seeming perplexed, and Gajus Runecaster not wanting the other to read the thoughts in his eyes. Neither of them spoke.

Two *twists* of the small hourglass later, a servant came to tell the count and the general that all preparations had been made. At the same time, the bell atop the red tower that stood in the middle of Alvon Keep rang exactly ten times. All within the keep left their assigned posts to spots where they could see the inner courtyard .

Alvon Keep was similar in size to the now-fallen fortress of Stafolos, but it boasted a larger garrison. Drawing their steeds, knights in solemn war-garb moved into formation in the courtyard, while behind them some of the hardiest keep guards lined up. It was a sight to behold.

In the Gohran military, one troop was comprised of roughly a hundred and fifty horsemen, who were then further divided into five squads. A full three troops of Count Ricard's red knights awaited in formation along with two squads of the white-armored knights who belonged to the general's personal guard.

The red knights stood in three lines. Upon their chests, standing out against the red of their breastplates, gleamed the crest of the Mongauli archduke, the scorpion of Mongaul combined with the lion of Gohra. Three troop captains with red plumes falling from their helms stood at the head of the lines, while behind them could be seen fifteen squad captains sporting shorter red plumes.

The two squads of white knights from Torus bore the same Mongauli crest. Their captains, Count Vlon and Baron Lindrot of Torus, wore white plumes in their helms similar in length to those of the troop captains of the red knights.

Amnelis appeared on the balcony, a page in tow bearing her jeweled sword. She looked down with some satisfaction at the forces assembled in the courtyard below. Nowhere among the men was there a glimmer of fear, a hesitant expression, or a face that betrayed any sign of weakness. But there was tension and excitement in those five hundred faces that now turned to look up with undisguised reverence at the archduke's daughter.

Even were she not their respected general, the sight of Amnelis would have stirred them. She had once again put on her white armor and a long cloak that hung from her shoulders. Sheathed at her waste was a shortsword with a jeweled hilt; she held her helm in her hands, letting her shining golden hair flow freely down her back. Her face was pale and shone with the purity of youth, bold yet beautiful, like that of a hero of legend. She nodded to her page and took the slim jeweled sword from him. Then she turned to the assembled knights and spoke.

"Tonight, these three troops of the red, together with the white knights led by Vlon and Lindrot, will make a crossing of the Kes River and enter Nospherus, where we will pursue and capture the twins of Parros and those who harbor them. I,

Amnelis, daughter to the archduke and General of the Right, will lead you personally. This night crossing and the ensuing expedition into Nospherus will be dangerous. Each troop of red will begin by lighting a bonfire from which to draw torches so that we may have light to see our surroundings and each other. You will carry three days' rations; we will return when our mission is accomplished. A reminder: I want none of you to leave your assigned squad for any reason, and all my orders are to be obeyed swiftly and without question."

"For Mongaul!" The cheering of the troops shook the walls of Alvon.

"We ride!" Amnelis lifted the jeweled sword in her hand toward the sky.

While the keep guard watched, the knights of the expedition mounted their horses. Amnelis disappeared from the balcony only to reappear soon afterwards among the ranks of warriors, her white cloak fluttering behind her as she lightly mounted the great white steed brought by her page.

The hulking, sour-faced Count Vlon and the compact Baron Lindrot rode up on either side of her, followed by the caster Gajus and a single mounted page. Led by Amnelis, these were the first to leave through the main gate of the keep, the white knights falling into rank behind them. Part of the keep guard, wearing only light armor, brought up the rear with Count Ricard at their head.

Twilight had come and gone; night had fallen on the Marches. Had the archduke's daughter not insisted on haste, not a man in the war party that now rode out of the gates would

have had to do anything as foolhardy as attempt a night crossing
of the Kes.

But the troops, elite soldiers of Mongaul, said not a word in
protest. Following their solemnly beautiful general, they rode
their horses out through the woods surrounding Alvon Keep.
They rode in five files, with all the knights on the flanks bearing
torches. As they progressed, the lights they bore illuminated the
path with a harsh and unaccustomed brightness. The knights
could see the creatures of the forest, disturbed from their
sleep—or their hunting—dashing from the half-lit underbrush
into the darkness of the forest beyond. Though few of the stout
knights paid any notice, there were a few unmistakable sighs of
relief when at last they came out of the wood to where they could
see the Kes below them. The river's waters were lit to shining by
the bluish-white light of Aeris Moongoddess—a strange glow
that made the water float in their eyes, like some phantasm of a
river, not real at all.

They stood now on the cliffs overlooking the river-gorge.
Behind them stretched the endless, black wood of Alvon, formless and foreboding in the dark except for the area around the
keep, where the watchfires of the guard cast a ring of light across
the surrounding treetops. Beyond that, too far to be seen even
in the bright moonlight lay the Roodwood, and in it the burnt
shell of Stafolos Keep.

The knights stood for a while, awaiting orders, looking
down at the glimmering river. It was deceptively placid, the
quiet lapping of the water against the rocks giving no hint of the
innumerable dangers that lurked within. Yet if the knights knew

the danger, as they surely did, they gave no sign. All stood silently, each helm lit on one side by the torchlight, and on the other side dark and formless.

Amnelis's white armor and the golden hair that flowed down her back was as a beacon to the troops, a star floating up out of the darkness before them.

"More torches."

Amnelis seemed to hesitate, perhaps knowing what awaited them in the waters below, but it was only for a moment. Her orders rang out clear in the night air. The knights hung their crossbows from their saddle-knobs where they could be quickly reached. Then they drew out the remaining torches they were carrying and lit them from the fires carried at the sides of the column. Soon it was bright as midday in a wide circle around them.

Amnelis raised a white-gloved hand and the knights began their descent down the narrow path to the river. The path switched back many times before reaching the riverbank. There was not enough room on the narrow way or the rocks below for all five hundred of the knights, so two squads of red knights went down first, dismounting and leading their horses by the bit.

Count Ricard's engineers had been busy making preparations, bringing rafts down to the riverbank. These craft were much like the raft the fugitives had used to escape from Stafolos, but better reinforced with iron and with railings built specifically for better defense.

Leaving their horses behind, the leading troops fixed torches to the rafts and boarded, ten men to a raft. Three rafts were pushed off from the shore by the engineers, and the knights used their poles to push out further onto the water.

Where Guin and the others had been content to let the current carry them down the river, the Mongauli troops were seeking to cross the waterway directly, and the task before them was much more demanding. It took ten poles on each raft to fight the current, dipping down so hard they scraped against the bottom in the shallows. As soon as they were afloat, the rafts began to rock, the light from the swaying torches on deck sending shadows darting out and back in deranged races across the water. Paying no attention to the other rafts, each group of ten concentrated all their efforts on scanning the water immediately around them for danger.

Suddenly a scream came from one of the rafts, followed by the sound of spraying water. Hands gripped swords instinctively.

"Bigmouth!"

From the shore, Count Ricard saw a plume of water shoot over a raft, dousing half of the torches. Sounds of battle came drifting over the water.

"First wave! Report casualties!" the count charged up to the water's edge and shouted.

For a while, there was only the clamor of men yelling to each other out on the raft. Finally the report came: the attack was over, with two casualties. The bigmouth had taken one, and the other had been knocked off the raft in a surge of spray.

"Permission to rescue the soldier in the river!" one of the knights shouted back to shore.

"Denied! The next rafts will look for him!" Ricard answered, though he knew the chances of finding anyone in the night river were slim, especially if he wore armor.

After what seemed an eternity, a raft made it to the opposite bank. The ten knights scrambled onto the safety of the shore with obvious relief, forgetting for a moment that they were now in the wildlands of Nospherus and probably in even more danger than they had been on the water.

They hauled their raft part way onto the shore and fastened it tightly to the rocks with chains and ropes. The other two rafts moored themselves in a similar fashion, one on either side of the first raft. Once the three vessels were secure, the knights groped in the water behind them for a set of chains that linked these rafts to another trio of rafts back on the Gohran side of the river. Then, using capstans with pegs to grip the chains, they began to pull the next three rafts across.

The going from there on was far easier than the first crossing had been. With the combined forces of poles and chains propelling them, the rafts slid quickly across the river. This wave of knights worked swiftly to fasten their rafts to the first ones with iron latches, then went to join the front guard on the Nospherus shore. The process was repeated ten times, until a line of linked rafts stretched across the whole of the river, forming a floating bridge of sorts. As a finishing touch, sturdy iron poles were fastened along the length of the bridge, stabilizing it against the tugging of the current and making it easier for the knights to cross. Though the undulating span was in constant motion and the footing precarious in places, the next squad was able to make the crossing on horseback in three lines.

The remaining red knights moved over the river quickly, leading the mounts of the men who had crossed the river steedless.

Amnelis watched with satisfaction as her men crossed the bridge. The first stage of the expedition was a complete. They had a bridge.

"Gajus, the time!"

"Three *twists* before sunrise, my Lady."

"Then we keep moving."

The red knights had finished the crossing, leaving only two squads of the white on the west bank. Amnelis turned towards Ricard.

"Return to the keep, leaving a platoon here to guard the bridge. At first light, I want you to send a company to the Nospherus side to build a wall as we discussed. Your engineers will reinforce the bridge. Send each other messengers twice daily, once at dawn, once at dusk, and use the watchfires as well. Let the reinforcements from Tauride rest well after they arrive, then have them cross over and establish a line of defense. Understood?"

"Yes, General. And please—be careful," said Ricard. His rugged voice had an undertone of genuine concern. "Nospherus is Doal's domain, and the Golden Scorpion Palace needs you."

"I will return to the makeshift fort when I have captured the fugitives. Should the waters rise before then and take down the bridge, rebuild it, as many times as you have to."

"Yes, General."

"And keep an eye on the situation at Stafolos…it is unlikely, but should the Sem attack again…"

"I understand."

Amnelis nodded. She put on her white helm, lowering the faceplate and tucking the billows of her golden hair carefully out of sight. Then she turned and called out to her captains, Vlon on her right and Lindrot on her left. "We cross!"

She rode down toward the bridge, her cloak gliding like a ghost behind her.

The white knights spurred their horses, and all began to make across the floating bridge as one. In their midst rode Gajus Runecaster. In his black-hooded cloak, atop a dun-maned mount with black trappings and a black saddle, he stood out like a spot of ink in a stream of milk.

The torches along the bridge rails create a false sense of security, thought Ricard as he watched the knights move across the unsteady planks. *Reckless, our general is…reckless and beautiful. Would that I were not charged to defend the keep! I would cross this foul river with her.*

With the keep guard standing watch, Amnelis and the sixty white knights crossed without incident. The red knights on the far bank waited, reins in hand, for the general's arrival. Then, without a moment's pause or rest, the expeditionary force began its journey into the wildlands of Nospherus.

In those days, the region known as the Marches, with its endless rocky deserts, its dark forests filled with creatures defying description, and its fey and barbarous tribes, far surpassed the Middle Country both in vastness and in the threats it posed.

To the folk of the Middle Country, who felt that they alone knew civilization, it seemed that the whole of humankind lived in the area bounded by the Marches and by the watery expanses of Lentsea and Corsea. Within these borders they fought over tiny patches of fertile land and built their kingdoms around them. The Middle Country extended for a few thousand tads between the Kes River in the east and the River Argo away to the southwest where lush green plains stretched down to the surf of the Lentsea. The warm and distant Southlands, embracing in their vastness mighty deserts and jungles and the sun-drenched islands of Simhara, Uranya, and Lodos floating in the Corsea, and the frigid Northlands, with their kingdoms etched out of ice, had all become but half-forgotten myths to the people of the Middle Country who knew little and cared less about the world beyond their brightly lit halls and crystal palaces.

The Henna Highroad or "The Red Road," so named for the ruddy cobblestones that paved its length, was the lifeblood of the Middle Country, allowing trade and communication between the various kingdoms, duchies, and free cities. In ages to come, the highroad was to extend to the farthest reaches of the Marches, but in the days of which this story tells it served only to connect the bustling cities of the Middle Country. The Marches, a deep and wild natural barrier against civilization, were left to homesteaders, rogues and pioneers.

The harsh borderlands seemed a peaceful garden compared to the savage terrain into which the expeditionary force was now riding. They were in the no-man's-land, heading east—in the direction the fugitives had gone the night before. During the first hours of their journey, knights glancing backward could still see the torches burning at the river-crossing near Alvon Keep like guardian spirits unwisely left behind.

There was nothing that might justly be called a road in Nospherus, only the sometimes mossy, mostly barren tracks that snaked between the massive stone boulders that cluttered the otherwise featureless landscape. The dark of night seemed deeper here, and only Doal Demongod knew what hideous beasts it hid.

Amnelis considered her situation. Around her, five hundred knights riding five abreast rode in silence with their torches lifted high. She knew that the torch-flames would announce their presence should the fugitives be close by, but to travel without lights in the night of the no-man's-land would be folly. The knights rode in close rank, each continually checking his fellow on his side, passing and relighting torches as they died or were blown out, holding their lights extended to illuminate the path where the footing was treacherous.

Despite the torches, the darkness here was more cloying, thicker than it had been on the river. It was almost as if the night itself were a living thing, an impure jelly-like life-form that flowed around them and consumed the light. And there were things moving in the blackness beyond the range of the torches, little whorls of blackness where the dark had coalesced into something terrible that hungered and that hated all intruders. There was no stillness in this night, it was filled with even more prowlers than the Roodwood.

Amnelis rode safely in the middle of the ranks, surrounded by five hundred mounted warriors. Still, as they rode, a scream like that of a weeping woman sounded directly over her hooded head, followed at once by a sound of great wings flapping. When the men lifted their torches high, whatever had made the sound was gone, but they caught a glimpse of something slimy on the ground scuttling out of the circle of light on thousands of tiny legs, some horrid cross between a leech and a centipede.

The foul denizens of Nospherus did not seem to disturb Amnelis. She appeared to be deep in thought as she gently guided her horse along, her faceplate lowered and her hood drawn over her head to hide her countenance.

Dawn should have been coming soon, yet still the darkness crawled along the ground and writhed between their horses' legs, and there was a foul odor in the air. It was an indescribable stench, like nothing the knights had smelled before. It clung in their nostrils and overwhelmed their other senses until there seemed to be nothing to see, or hear, or feel, but only the stench to struggle against. It seemed to bother the caster Gajus the most. He had drawn his hood over his head and pulled the edge of his cloak over his face and mouth to filter the air. As he rode swaying on his horse, he muttered to himself in a voice too low to be intelligible to others.

This stench, it is that of the crawlers—or no, it is the land-dwelling cousin of the bigmouth...it bodes ill, very ill! But the stars led my Lady here; it was the choice of fate; she was meant to come...

In truth, the stars had weighed very heavily on his mind

since he glimpsed their strange movements in his divination sphere back at the keep. There were too many factors, too much juxtaposition for him to discern whether the celestial lights foretold good or evil. What a tangled skein was being woven in the heavens above them! And its pattern was only now beginning to take shape.

There were only a few diviners that could possibly read the message of these stars clearly—the sage Locandross, oracle of the west, or perhaps the acharya Agrippa, who had lived for twenty thousand years (it was said) and still drew breath! And of course, there was Glateis, the Dark Celebrant himself. Compared to them, with their long-cultivated powers of divination, Gajus was but a new-hatched gosling with his head in the mud. Yet these stars would prove a worthy challenge even for the elders; Agrippa might need to spend his next two or three thousand years just looking at them before he knew what they told. Gajus guessed that there was none other than these three—each at the pinnacle of the sorcerous arts—that could offer true insight into the riddles in the sky.

Perhaps what I should do is go seek them out? But no! What am I saying? Mulberries! Mulberries! Is the Dark Celebrant Glateis not the highest priest in Doal's own dark order? To court such a power would be folly! And Agrippa, the legendary acharya, powerful sorcerer and diviner of truths? He is more legend than truth, I fear, and his whereabouts unknown, if indeed he exists at all. Just finding him would be a quest worthy of an epic sung by kitara players throughout the land. Were I to visit any of them, it would have to be the sage Locandross. He is a white mage, and a diviner of the heavens. But there again, they say that he has gone off deep into the mountains and spends his nights gaz-

ing at the stars, alone, unconcerned about the troubles of this world; rarely is he seen of late. For all I know, he may have died out there, his glassy eyes fixed forever on the whirling polestar...

Gajus shivered mightily. It would be most difficult, most difficult indeed, but then he was wrong to expect that Jarn Fateweaver would go out of his way to spin a design that was easy to read for the sake of curious mortals. *It is all I can do,* thought Gajus, *to make sure that the thread my Lady walks is the right one. But with the crawlers and the bigmouths and that horrid stench—it is not clear at all that any of these five hundred will return to Alvon unharmed, if they return at all! This shall be most difficult...most difficult indeed!*

"Gajus!" The general's sharp whip-crack of a voice broke through the diviner's thoughts. "Must you mumble so?"

"Aaa..." croaked the diviner.

Amnelis turned away from the sullen diviner, whose head now drooped even further down toward his horse's neck. She pulled back her hood and lifted her faceplate to better survey their surroundings.

The thick darkness of the night was finally beginning to lift. Gradually, the edges of a mountain range to the east became visible, painted a faint orange in the growing light, and the sky began to peel off the black of night in thin layers, as if strips of paper were lifting to reveal the translucent whites and grays of the wildlands.

After a while, Amnelis gave the order to put out the torches.

Baron Lindrot edged his horse up towards the general's. He spoke softly. "My Lady, if I may, are we sure this is the direction in which the fugitives went? Might we not cover more ground if we split into two or three groups?"

Amnelis waved his question aside with a white-gloved hand. "Gajus's divining board has shown that they went toward Kanan in the east. Once the night lifts we may send a scouting patrol to the top of one of these outcroppings to search for any sign of them. But we will proceed as one. I do not wish to divide our forces in the lands of Nospherus."

"Yes, my Lady."

"Tell each of the commanders to ride back along the lines and make sure there are none missing."

Lindrot saluted and nudged his white horse towards the front of the lines. Soon, the orders were passed down through the commanders, and once again there was movement among the ranks as the weary soldiers came out of the long, dreary gloom of the night.

There were no stragglers. Satisfied, Amnelis waited until they had drawn abreast of a small rocky hill to their left, where she ordered the troops to halt for the first time since they had made the river crossing.

"We will rest here for one *twist*. Dismount, feed your horses, and take turns napping. I want no more than half of you asleep at one time, and even then stay clad in your armor, ready to ride at a moment's notice should I give the order."

After this was passed down the line, Amnelis signaled to her captains Vlon and Lindrot, and to Gajus and his page, to follow her on horseback up a rocky hillside.

The general's white horse seemed glad that the long night was finally over, and he lifted his hooves high as he galloped with ease up the rocky incline. Amnelis only reined the animal to a halt once they had reached a flat stretch of ground on the very top of the hill. Then, still mounted and holding the reins in one hand, she surveyed the vast expanse of Nospherus.

A sigh escaped her lips. As far as she could see in all directions stretched an ocean of white and ash. The undulating rocks that stuck out of the swirling sands were like the crests of waves—only the foul mists that rose here and there from the pallid ground broke the illusion that she was standing on an island in the sea. Though the sun had not yet risen, the peaks of the mountains in the distance were lit by a fiery glow, and the wildlands were slowly growing brighter with each passing moment. Yet there were no birds here to warm the heart with their song, no woodland creatures to cry out the beginning of the day.

As she stood staring out over the wildlands a red glow crept slowly over the sands until all was the color of blood, and the sun rose, far more lurid than it ever seemed on the plush side of the Kes. So day began in Nospherus.

Faint wisps of white angel hair came blowing on a light wind, wrapping around the faces and armor of the general and the four men behind her, only to dissolve a moment later.

Amnelis's eyes narrowed.

She lifted a hand and pointed out and downward, to the east.

There, from the shadow of a clump of boulders, rose a thin wisp of smoke.

Amnelis lowered her faceplate and lightly rapped her horsewhip across the neck of her mount. At once her strong steed wheeled and charged back down the rocky slope at full gallop. The others hurried to keep up. They had found their fugitives.

—— 3 ——

"Guin...please, I need to rest. I don't think I can walk one more step." Rinda, panting heavily, collapsed on a small rock to the side of the path. Remus trudged over and sat down beside her.

How far had they run? Their raft had splintered on the boulders, and the knights were yelling from the other shore, ordering them to come back. One of the crossbow shots meant to warn them hit a rock right next to Remus. The drenched companions had started running, and never looked back.

By the time the twins' legs were threatening to give out from exhaustion, the sun had long since fallen below the horizon, and the night was thick about them. Guin and Istavan exchanged glances—even the hardened mercenary's shoulders were heaving. He sat down without waiting for Guin's nod of approval.

"We'll be fine, nobody's going to cross the Kes River by night on horseback!" the soldier declared, catching his breath as he pulled a vasya fruit from the leather satchel at his waist. Eagerly he began to eat. Their gati—the ground flour balls used as rations in the Marches—and the dried meat they carried had all been soaked in the noxious waters of the Kes and had become inedible.

For a short while the companions rested in silence, Suni and the twins breathing heavily and rubbing their tired legs. After a time Istavan looked up from his fruit. "Let's make a fire," he suggested. Guin looked as though he was going to stop him, but Istavan waved his hand. "I told you, we'll be fine. Or do you plan on spending a night in Nospherus huddling here in the dark?"

Guin had to agree, the mercenary had a point. They went about collecting armfuls of dried moss and soon had enough to start a fire. It was small, but, gathered around its warm light, they felt safe for the first time since the attack on the river.

"Well, well, well." Istavan, who had to be the first to comment on anything, spoke as he chewed on his vasya fruit. "Our raft is a fine bundle of bigmouth toothpicks, and we're being chased by the Gohran army. This puts a bit of a damper on our plans, eh?"

Rinda snuggled up next to Remus and pulled Suni close beside her. She stared at the fire. Somehow, sitting here stroking Suni's furry head, she could forget where she was and everything that had happened to them. And looking at Guin— the firelight illuminated half of his leopard face, strange and powerful as a myth—she felt that even if she had no one else to turn to, she was safe here with him.

Istavan's chattering continued: "Well, we can't go back to Gohra, that's for certain. Especially without a raft. Then again, we're not going to have an easy time making it through the no-man's-land as unprepared as we are. Flaming torqrats! Jarn's really got it in for us this time. Unless you got a plan, leopard-man?"

"Maybe," muttered Guin, "but it's not worth talking about now. Our path is clear: we cannot turn back, so we must go forward."

"Hunh!" Istavan scoffed, and sounded as though he was going to tease Guin again when he made a choking noise and waved his hand as though he was brushing something away from him.

Rinda looked up. "What's wrong?"

"Doal! Blasted angel hair! Stuff came floating up and stuck to my face while I was talking."

"Be careful," Guin warned. "Angel hair is harmless enough in small amounts, but if enough of it gets on you, it'll go up your nose and choke you to death. Those floating strands are the most common living things here in Nospherus."

"You seem to know a lot about this place," said Istavan, sullenly. "And why not? You came from here, didn't you? You're probably happy to be home, eh?"

"Why do you keep saying that? You don't know Guin's from Nospherus!" Rinda protested.

"'Cause every freak's from Nospherus, little girl," said the mercenary. "But that doesn't help us now. So! We go forward. Fair enough. Care to let me know how you plan to keep us alive while we're doing that? And tell me also where exactly we're headed out here in the middle of this no-man's-land without enough food even to make a single decent meal? To Kanan?"

"Yes."

"You know how many tads there are between here and the Kanan Mountains?"

"I think so."

"So let me get this straight." Istavan began to draw in the sand with the point of his knife. "We cross over the Kanan Mountains—just a few ranges of pathless mountains. Fine. Simple as whacking a louse. Then there are the jungles and the rivers to cross; and once we've done that, we have to make our way through the strange countries of the Eastlands and find a ship to take us to Cheironia. That all part of your plan?"

"I see no other way."

"Okay, let's get started then," said the mercenary with forced gaiety. "That would take a soldier on foot...hmm, about a year without rest. Even assuming we eat what's left of this scrawny Sem girl—"

"Istavan!" Rinda's eyes opened wide and she hugged Suni to her protectively. "Y-You can't eat Suni! Barbarian! Beast!" Shocked, she could barely get the words out straight.

Istavan's black eyes twinkled mischievously. "You don't eat monkeys where you're from? In Valachia, we used to roast them on festival days...mmm! Now *that* was a feast!"

Rinda, realizing too late that she was being teased, bit her lip and fell silent, glowering. Suni looked back and forth between the humans as though she half-understood what was being said. Then she wriggled her way out of Rinda's embrace and went over to Guin, where she began chittering loudly in a high, worried tone.

Guin tilted an ear towards Suni. With an air of surprise, he began to talk back to her in the same high staccato language. Suni responded, more urgently than before.

"Hey, Guin. What's that monkey chattering on about?"

"Don't call her a monkey, you—"

Guin raised a hand to silence the indignant princess. "Suni says she does not forget the life-debt she owes. She says it is dangerous to wander Nospherus this way. We should go to her village. The Raku tribe will thank us and give us safe passage through Sem territory to wherever we wish to go."

"Really, Suni? You can help us?" Rinda's face melted into a smile and she enfolded Suni in a joyful hug. The little Sem girl chirped and returned the embrace.

"The Sem, save us?" Istavan looked incredulous. "By the fiery tongue of Doal, I've never heard a finer idea. Why don't we just run ourselves through with our swords right now and save the fiends the trouble, eh?"

"Really!" Rinda glared at the mercenary. "To use the Dark One's name so freely, and on his very doorstep no less! You shouldn't swear so, or you'll have us all suffer for your impudence!"

"Hah! You don't get anywhere as a mercenary hiding your head under a rock every time someone says 'Doal'! Why, in the betting pits of Valachia, that's one of the nicer words you hear!"

"My!" Rinda hastily made the sign of Janos. Both the twins looked genuinely shocked. "If we weren't already in the wildlands of Nospherus I'd say you'd cursed this journey! Why, you'd curse any journey!"

Istavan grinned. "You might not be too far off. You know they call me Istavan Spellsword, the Crimson Mercenary of Valachia, but there are some who call me by another name: Istavan Calamity-Caller. The man who brings trouble wherever he goes." Istavan's voice rang with a sort of brash, perverse pride.

Remus grimaced. "I can believe it."

Chuckling, Istavan went on to elaborate. "That's why, wherever I go, noble lads pick fights with me and get killed, while proper ladies have affairs with me and are thrown out of both court and house...and even great castles fall, like Stafolos, eh? My talent, of course, lies in the fact that no matter what calamity I bring about, I'm able to escape by the skin of my neck. I'm the only one that seems immune to the calamities I bring! I think that's got to be some sort of divine power, don't you? Someone's watching over me, and it's not high holy Janos or that old geezer Jarn. No, I think the big bad guy Doal himself is looking out for Istavan, and as allies go, that's none too shabby."

Remus's face was pale. "Why don't you just sell your soul to Doal right now! Your jesting is—"

Remus stopped. Guin and Istavan seemed transfixed; even Suni sat motionless. Everyone was looking at Rinda.

A change had come over her. Her face, gleaming in the light of the campfire, had ceased to be her face at all. Gone was the youthful innocence that had played among her noble features. There was a new power there, and she was a true princess now, almost holy, like a shrine maiden at the temple of Janos. Her eyes were dark and shimmering, and looked as though they held the wisdom of a thousand years. The others held their breath and waited for her to speak.

Rinda lifted a hand, her movements seeming too graceful and measured for one so young. She pointed at the mercenary from Valachia.

"Soon..." Rinda's voice was not her own; it had become older, hoarser, wiser, and almost terrifying. "Soon, you will know, o bringer of great calamity, you will know that misfortune does not spare the messenger. Your disaster is always near by, and it will come to you in time. When the Lionstar rises victorious, bright enough to erase the star of your misfortune from the sky...only then will you know peace. All of the Middle Country suffers the calamity you carry on your endless wanderings...it will not release its grip until your star fades in the dawning light...it...

"You will know that the light of that unlucky star falls on you, too."

Her pale eyelids closing like heavy shutters over her eyes, Rinda slumped abruptly, the strength seeming to run from her body. She leaned onto Remus beside her.

"What was that?" Istavan began, ready to have some fun at the seer's expense, but he could not find the words to continue. It was not fear, but a strange kind of numbness that had come over the young mercenary, as though he had witnessed an eternity that stretched forever, too vast to comprehend. He stared at

Rinda.

Here, in this corner of the no-man's-land night, it seemed that time and space had stopped and tilted all their weight upon him. The gloom was never-ending and the night showed no signs of breaking. An intense loneliness came over Istavan, a feeling of isolation that froze his heart. He looked around confused. He was searching for someone, anyone, a living body, an inhabitant of the world of man. What he saw instead was a darkness and night that gave him no respite from the eternal void. Floating before him was the face of the otherworldly shrine maiden who spoke of his fate, her eyes half-closed like those of a mask. Across from her the half-man half-beast warrior sat erect, her guardian angel he seemed, or perhaps an idol from some bizarre cult.

The faces of the Sem girl and the heir to the throne of Parros were swallowed in darkness, so that all he could see were the leopard-headed warrior and the young Farseer who seemed to Istavan's eyes disturbingly close right then to being a goddess.

And time stretched on forever—

Istavan shuddered. The young, reckless mercenary had been promised an unusual fortune from birth, and it had given him an indefatigable sense of humor and self-assurance, but now he could not stop trembling. How many blood-curdling adventures had he seen? Was he not invulnerable—the Spellsword? Still...

Time was stopped, frozen. This was a place which those in the hands of fate, mortal men doomed someday to die, should not trespass—should not even look. The chill tremors that crept from the bottom of Istavan's soul and shook his body like a leaf were nothing more than a manifestation of his realization that he was seeing what he should not be seeing. He did not belong there!

"I..." Istavan pried his tongue from where it was stuck to the roof of his mouth and made to say something. Then, in the campfire, a brand split with a loud crack, sending sparks up into the night air.

The spell was broken. The campfire wavered, and time began to flow again. In the light of the fire were four creatures of flesh and blood, all walking the threads of Jarn's loom, all mortal.

Istavan quietly took a deep breath. He exhaled, trying to get out the last of that horrid feeling of loneliness that had come over him a moment before. *Get a grip, Istavan!*

Guin leaned forward and prodded the fire. The lack of expression on his leopard features made it seem as if he had not even noticed the anomalous moment. He turned his shining yellow eyes towards the others and spoke.

"When dawn comes, they will send riders after us. That is what I would do, were I lord of Alvon. It is certain that they have made a connection between our presence on the river and the fall of Stafolos, and if their eyes are sharp, they may have seen Suni. Should they then think that we are part of some raiding party, enemies of Gohra returning to our Sem allies, they may come in great force indeed. It may be dangerous to travel by night in the no-man's-land, yet travel we must. We need to put more distance between us and the river."

"Yeah...yeah, you've got a point," Istavan agreed. There was still a trace of the chill in his voice, but he quickly perked up. "We should get moving. But what I'm still wondering is what Torus white knights are doing in the red knight territory of Alvon. Something fishy is going on, I'll bet my sword on it."

"Do not wager your sword, we will need it," Guin growled. "We must make haste to find a place where we can hide. Then we can plan what to do next."

"Plan?"

"Yes. We cannot run from the Gohran forces forever. They cast a wide net, and their scouts' eyes are well trained."

"You saying we should fight back?" Istavan scoffed, giving Guin an incredulous look. He seemed to have forgotten entirely the strangeness of a few moments before. "By the long forked tongue of Jarn, what do you intend to accomplish against the might of Gohra?"

"What will you do in Cheironia?"

"Well, I was thinking I could find some warlord, pass the tests, and disappear among the ranks of his mercenaries."

"That may be fine for you, but what about Guin?" Rinda demanded. Her face had gone back to being that of a young girl. Gone was the mysterious, divine coldness that had surrounded her when she spoke just moments before. It was as if her brief transformation had been no more than a dream. "How do you expect him to just disappear among a bunch of soldiers looking like he does? He would be caught, and questioned, and sentenced to some horrible fate! And what about Remus and me?" Rinda bit her quivering lip.

The mercenary grinned. This was familiar territory! "Listen, I have enough trouble just watching out for myself. I can't go worrying about every freak that happens along, and besides, I think he's perfectly able to look after himself."

Guin nodded, cutting off another outburst from Rinda.

"The mercenary is right, I can look after myself. But we are in the middle of Nospherus, and there are many, many tads of travel between us and the nearest civilization, unless we are to return to Gohra, which would be walking into the lion's maw. Tell me, Istavan, are you wholly against asking these Raku tribe Sem for their strength?"

"Their strength? I thought we were talking about a guide out of here." Istavan smiled wryly and brushed the black hair out of his beady eyes. This boyish gesture reminded Rinda of how young he was—barely twenty years of age. He'd be almost handsome if he weren't so incredibly annoying.

"What's going on in that leopard head of yours, I wonder? You don't mean to suggest that we join up with those monkey tribes and invade the Archduchies of Gohra, do you? I thought that mask of yours was making the Sem girl sweet on you, but maybe it works both ways, eh?"

Istavan slapped his knee and laughed until he had to wipe the tears from his eyes—an innocent display of mirth, but one that did not amuse Rinda. "Istavan! Of all the crude vagabonds I have ever heard of, you are the most insulting!" She chastised the still-laughing mercenary, not realizing that her anger was giving him more cause for mirth.

"If he doesn't want to go with us, let him do as he pleases," said Remus, eager to avoid yet another argument. "Guin, we'll go with you to Suni's village. I don't know about any invasion, but maybe they can help us get to Earlgos or Cheironia. We could hide there until we find some remnants of the armies of the crystal city, and—"

"Remus!" Rinda cut her brother off, but it was too late. Istavan's almond-shaped eyes widened, then just as swiftly narrowed. The mercenary chewed his lower lip with a satisfied look.

"Ah-hah. I knew there was something unusual about you two!" Istavan pointed at each of the twins in turn. "Let's see...that would make you, and you, the orphans of Parros. So you survived the fires of the Black Dragon War!"

"Remus, you idiot!" Rinda hissed. Her violet eyes burned with an indignant rage, but they were glaring at the Crimson Mercenary. "That is correct, mercenary. I am the prophetess Rinda, of the true holy line of Parros. And this is indeed my brother, the sole heir to the throne. So now you know. What of it? Sell us to Gohra if you will, simply run back and tell them where we are. I'm sure those at Alvon Keep would overlook your desertion if you did. Why, they might even make you a knight. But you would be cursed from here to eternity by the royal line of Parros and all those faithful to it! Go ahead—choose!"

"Now just hold on, little lady," began Istavan with a wry smile. He didn't want to admit it himself, but bearing the full force of Rinda's wrath head-on like this was enough to make even his ready wit reel back in temporary retreat. At the same time he couldn't help admire the beauty of her flashing violet eyes, and her proud cheeks, scarlet with rage. She was a princess, all right. Of course, he was as stubborn and cantankerous as they came, and he had a mind to let her know that.

"State your intentions, Crimson Mercenary!" Rinda demanded, heedless of his internal conflict. "There is little we can do. We cannot kill you to keep you silent, as much as we would like to, and there is not much that two orphans without throne or country can offer in the way of rewards or favors. All we have is our royal blood and our pride. We are powerless! What would you do with us? Speak!"

"Well…" Istavan chewed on his lip. His initial satisfaction at having learned the royal twins' identity had been replaced by unease as he realized the weightiness of the situation.

Guin slowly stood, his eyes on the mercenary as he spoke to Rinda. "My Princess! You are not as powerless as you may think. While you may have lost your armies, you have a faithful knight by your side, and it would be a simple matter for him to reach out with his bare hands and twist the neck of any traitor that might seek to sell you to your enemies."

"Hey Guin…" Istavan protested.

Rinda and Remus rushed to the side of the leopard-headed warrior. "Guin!" Rinda, forgetting all her royal pride, buried her face under the curve of his powerful arm and wept for joy.

The leopard warrior did not move to comfort them nor push them away. Instead, he fixed his yellow gaze more intently on Istavan standing across the campfire.

"Don't cry, Rinda." Remus rubbed his sister's shoulder. Below, Suni grabbed onto Rinda's leg and stared up with a fixed expression of worry.

Istavan couldn't decide whether to laugh out loud or to scream in exasperation. Finally, he slammed a fist into the open palm of his other hand and cursed so loudly that Rinda stopped crying and turned around.

"By the fat arse of Janos that spreads over the realms of this world and the next, what's gotten into you people? From now on, I'll have to remind myself never to throw my lot in with miserable little girls and leopard-headed freaks. When did I, Istavan Spellsword, ever say I was going to sell any orphans, royal or no, to the Gohrans? By the black bladder of Doal! How can I get you to trust me? Suppose I just stay with you, eh? Would that satisfy you? Nice and close, every bleeding minute? You can scrub my arse and tuck me under my camp blanket at night. Then you'll know that I'm not off selling your secrets. Fine! Lead on! To the stinking monkey village or the far heights of Kanan, wherever! Take me to the den of Doal, or to bed with the wildlings, I don't care, damn it!"

Guin grunted once in approval, and turned his leopard head to the campfire. He concluded quietly, "We should leave as soon as we may. I will ask Suni how far it is to her tribe's village."

The warrior spoke with the tiny Sem in her language for a while, then addressed the others again. "She says it's a full day-and-a-half's journey—but that is on Sem legs. For us, perhaps a day at most."

"I hope she's right," Istavan replied. "We've only a bite of vasya fruit left among us, and our water is nearly gone. If we don't get more food—even stinking wildling grubs—I swear I'll eat our furry little friend."

"You just try it!" snapped Rinda. Guin held up his hand to silence her.

"Let us leave then. Make torches from the campfire. We head east."

It was as though an unspoken agreement had been made that the group would follow Guin's orders. Quickly they stood and made ready to leave, lighting torches and then dousing their fire. Soon, preparations were complete, and they set out into the gloom, moving as one—the leopard-headed warrior Guin, Istavan of Valachia, the twins of Parros, and Suni of the Raku tribe of the Sem—five companions bound by the will to survive.

—— 4 ——

The five fugitives traveled quickly, spurred on by an anxiety that might have been abject fear if they had known how closely they were being pursued. The riders from Alvon Keep were just then crossing the Kes on their floating bridge. But not even Istavan could have guessed that the archduke's daughter, the Lady Amnelis herself, was leading them. Such a bold move was beyond all expectation.

Nor did the companions have the benefit of horses as their pursuers did, though in this rugged landscape the lack of steeds was not a tremendous handicap, especially as they had the advantage of a local guide in the little Sem girl, Suni. Even in the depth of night she was able to steer them clear from most danger.

But the wildlands of Nospherus were no paradise even for the Sem who made it their home, and Suni was frequently compelled to stop to get her bearings in the darkness. The way she did this was quite fascinating to the twins. The little Sem would step off to the side of the path and fish around through the night air until she had snagged a few strands of the faintly luminescent angel hair that floated around them. Then she would hold it so that it trailed upon the wind. The angel hair would rapidly dissolve in the heat of her grasp, but Suni seemed to be able to discern what she needed to know in those few short moments.

Try as they might, the twins could not see how the wispy, phantom-like strands indicated anything. Though they hurt their eyes staring into that strange, bluish-white glow, the primitive life-forms would always melt away before they could figure out just what it was that Suni was looking at.

"I could understand it if these things ate," said Istavan, brushing off a tuft of angel hair that had blown against his cheek, "but all they do is just float around. It's creepy, I say. Aye, this whole place is damned, from the dirty Sem to the dullard Lagon. If the land-dwelling bigmouths don't get you, the sand-worms will...or maybe it'll be the flesh-eating nurls that look just like rocks until they lash out with teeth the size of longswords and rip you in two. The blood moss will soak up what's left of you." Istavan pawed away another clump of the glowing strands that had started to wrap around his leg. "Or maybe the angel hair will just bore you to death."

The mercenary gave an exaggerated yawn and looked around to see if anyone was listening to him. Undaunted by an apparent lack of audience, he continued. "This place sure is a nest of monstrosities. The kitara players have it right, this land's been hell on earth since its very creation. You know what they say? When Janos and Doal gambled for ownership of the world, and Janos won, he forgot to include Nospherus in his list of place names, and so Doal took it! That's why this is Doal's only domain in this world. But what a domain! I feel like I might go stark raving mad." He looked around at the others. "Then again, all my companions are either mad or monsters themselves, so maybe they'd start liking me better...Gack!"

Istavan coughed up a clump of angel hair that had managed to slip into his mouth while he was talking. "Blasted throat worms! Any more of this and a man won't even be able to whistle a little marching song to keep his feet moving. Ach, and when the sun comes up it'll turn this land into the bottom of a frying pan. By the six sides of the die that Janos and Doal rolled to play for the fate of the world, this place might just see the end of the Crimson Mercenary."

"Don't talk so much, you'll get thirsty," warned Guin in a low rumble.

Istavan licked his lips. "If there's anything worse than walking through this Doal-damned gloom, it's walking through it in silence. How do you expect to keep our spirits up with nothing but this blasted night to keep us company? It's depressing!"

"Keep chatting and we won't hear anything approach us. Better depressed than dead."

That seemed to give Istavan pause, and he fell silent for a while. But soon he was grumbling again, wanting Suni to find him some plant or animal to eat to stop the rumbling in his stomach. "I can wait until the sun comes up, I can wait until then, but not much longer or I'll collapse on the spot. I'd even eat some stinking Sem grubs if you asked me to. Come on, leopard-head, talk to this girl in that lovely chirping language and ask her if there's anything to eat around here. Do you mind?"

Guin growled and spoke to Suni, who listened and seemed to be thinking hard about the matter.

"Didn't you eat a whole vasya fruit a while back without giving us so much as a bite?" Rinda pointed out.

The mercenary furrowed his brow. "That stringy fruit's no more a meal than a pile of Doal's droppings. Ah, I've gone and said another bad word before the holy princess of Parros! Shame on me!" Istavan turned and spat into the darkness with practiced force.

"Imeeru!" Suddenly, Suni broke off her conversation with Guin and ran back to Istavan, jumping up to slap him on the chest, a scornful expression on her small face.

"What? What is it, you crazy monkey?" Istavan made to pick up the little girl and throw her bodily away from him, when he shrieked. "H-Help! *The dark has got me!*"

"Hiiii!" Suni jumped away, as did the twins.

It was indeed as if the darkness itself was attacking. Like some lacquer-black soup, the gloom to the side of the path had boiled into the light and was now attaching itself to Istavan's right leg.

Istavan shouted and grabbed his leg. Before he could draw his sword, the thing had engulfed him up to the knee. Now he hesitated, not relishing the thought of accidentally chopping off his own leg. The same risk stayed Guin's hand as well.

"Argh! It's coming farther up!" Istavan dropped to the ground and tried to scrape off the black gel that had now reached his waist. "Help me! Do something! How can you just stand there?"

Rinda reached out a hand to help, but Guin swiftly pushed her aside.

"Don't touch it—it's a yidoh, very dangerous."

"But he's going to die!"

"Stand back!"

Guin sprang into action, sweeping down to grab the mercenary by his afflicted right leg and hoisting it up into the air.

"Cover your face, this is going to be hot." Guin swung the torch in his other hand down toward the shapeless monster.

"Agh, Guin, you'll roast me alive!"

Heedless, Guin thrust the torch into the seething black mass.

Rinda screamed. Flames shot up around Istavan's right leg until he was a giant human torch. The strange jell-like creature burned and sputtered in the flame.

"Ahh, stop! It's too hot, too hot!" Istavan wailed like a child. "Water! Somebody put me out!"

"Guin! We don't have water! He'll die!" Remus held up an empty waterskin in panic. Without a pause, Guin pushed Istavan to the ground and thrust the mercenary's burning leg into the sand at the side of the path, and threw himself down on top of it.

"No! Guin!"

There was a rancid smell of burning flesh, and Rinda, feeling faint, sat down with her hands over her face. Guin's leopard head rolled back and he gave a low growl.

"Good," he said at last, and stood.

Istavan still lay in the sand, dazed. From his waist to his right foot, he was covered with the carcass, grimy and burned, of the yidoh. Yet his long leather boot seemed unharmed, and nowhere was there a sign of a wound or blood.

"Guin! Are you okay?" cried Rinda, running to him.

The warrior raised a hand and brushed away charred yidoh remains from his chest.

Rinda looked at his broad chest and exclaimed with horror, "Guin! You're burned! Why did you have to put out the fire like that?"

"It's nothing. I was wounded far worse in Randoch, and many—" he stopped in mid-utterance.

"Guin, what did you say? Y-You've remembered something! Randoch? Is that where you're from?" Rinda asked, agitated for his sake.

The leopard-man, forgetting all about the burn, was lost in intense thought for a moment, then shook his head. "It's no good."

"Remus? Did they ever teach you anything about a place called Randoch?"

"Well, there's Rangart, in the Duchy of Kaulos, and the free port city of Rygorl..." Remus said dubiously, recalling half-remembered geography lessons.

"What about you, Istavan?" Rinda turned to the mercenary, who still lay in the dirt. "You've been places, right?"

"Please, girl, have some pity for Doal's sake!" Istavan lurched to his feet with a look of outrage on his face. "I'm dying over here, and all you care about is leopard-head's washed-out memories?"

"Guin just saved you, didn't he? And it was your fault in the first place that you got attacked!"

"How was I supposed to know it was out there? What, could you see it? By the slimy scales of Doal's tail, I hope I never chance upon another one of *those* things. When it grabbed me I lost all feeling in my leg, I did. It was so cold...I thought I'd had it."

Suni chattered and Guin translated, a smile in his voice. "She says you brought it upon yourself. The yidoh are vicious when provoked, but they're not as aggressive as some other denizens of the wildlands, the bigmouths and the sandworms being just two. It only attacked because you spit on it. It must have thought you were food."

Istavan muttered a curse under his breath.

"You were lucky I got fire on it so quickly," added Guin. "You can't cut a yidoh off with swords or knives. Unless you burn it off, it will stay attached to its unconscious prey and slowly digest it."

"How do you know that?" Rinda asked in a whisper. "Not that much about you surprises me anymore."

"I just knew it. Something in my head said, *Fire—fire is the only way*."

Rinda shook her head and lightly brushed the dirt off Guin's wounded chest. "Are you sure you're okay?"

Guin nodded. "Are we all here?"

"Suni?" Rinda turned around to see the little Sem girl walking out of the darkness, which was slowly lifting now with the approach of dawn. Her hands were full of something.

"She says she found some moss nearby to use as a poultice; it can take the heat off the burn. Thank you, Suni." Guin nodded to the little girl, and bound some of the cool moss to his chest with a strip of cloth.

"About this Randoch," came the voice of the Crimson Mercenary from behind, just as Guin was getting ready to continue walking.

Everyone turned around. Istavan was looking off to the side of the trail, as if determined not to meet their eyes. "I'm sure I've heard that name somewhere before."

"Where? Is it a country? A town? Or maybe—" pressed the princess.

"That's what I'm trying to remember! Don't you ever shut up?" Istavan snapped at her. Then he slapped his knee. "That's it! Did I ever tell you I was on the crew of a Valachian trading ship in the Lentsea until I was fifteen?"

"A pirate ship, more likely."

Istavan smiled, letting the comment slide, which convinced Rinda all the more that she was right.

"Well, we encountered a mysterious ship on one of our voyages. It had a strange shape, long and sleek. It was swifter than any ship I'd seen before. It was all white and elegant. We thought for sure it had to be the ship of some king or noble. But when we were maneuvering to board it, it took off and disappeared, just like that, over the horizon." Istavan, realizing his admission, stuck out his tongue and grinned sheepishly. "Well, when we were making our first approach, I saw some writing on the white ship's bow: *Randoch*, it said."

"The name of the boat?" offered Remus.

"Maybe—and maybe not. That's just what I saw. And one other thing. There was a statue adorning the bow, the bust of a woman, and mighty pretty at that, with wings like a harpy. How about it, Guin? That other word you remember sounded like a woman's name."

"Aurra?"

Istavan nodded silently. For a brief time everyone was lost in thought, but not the kind that yields answers.

"Maybe Guin was the king of this Randoch," said Rinda, "and rebels put the curse of the leopard mask on him."

"You sure have an active imagination, girl," Istavan snorted. "Maybe you used to stay up all night worrying about rebels when you still had your kingdom?"

Istavan seemed not to care that Remus was glaring death at him. "It's strange. I'd completely forgotten about that spooky boat for a good five years, and now that one word from leopard-head brought it all back."

As he talked, they began walking again, each falling in line behind Guin, paying little heed to the approach of daylight. The eastern sky grew pale with warm light, the first sign of the blistering shadeless heat of day that was soon to come to the barren wildlands.

They stopped to rest, just for an hour. Tired and hungry, they tried chewing on some grassy-smelling moss that Suni found, but it only made their saliva flow and their stomachs rumble. They took turns napping; Istavan only had to look at Guin's wounds once to offer to take first watch. So it was that while the others slept, the mercenary sat on the lookout for any signs of unwanted guests, occasionally throwing dried moss onto the campfire.

He didn't even know what he'd do if another one of those sticky black jelly things showed up. Now that had been a shock! *If leopard-head hadn't come up with that little bit of wildlands lore when he did, I'd have cut off my own leg. Some 'Spellsword' I'd be! What a warrior this Guin is—he'd give Ruah a good fight, no mistake. By Mos' white goat beard, I'm glad he's on my side! Those twins, on the other hand...*

Mumbling and grumbling, the young mercenary reached into the wide cuff of his boot, where he had kept a last vasya fruit hidden, and began eating it, cursing under his breath as he chewed.

The sun crept steadily higher into the sky. Suddenly, Istavan jumped to his feet. "What's that? I sense—danger!" He spit the remainder of the vasya onto the ground. The hair on the back of his neck was rising and that could only mean one thing: enemies were nearby. "But that can't be...Wait..."

On the top of a nearby rocky crag, something sparkled in the morning sun. It was the white armor and golden hair of Amnelis, perched atop the hill to survey the area. She had just spotted their campfire.

Istavan's eyes narrowed, and he turned to wake the others, then stopped. Slowly he licked his lips as he made up his mind. Grinning, he gathered up his belongings around him and strapped on his sword belt. He looked over at the leopard-headed warrior, fast asleep, probably weak from his burn. The twins lay sprawled by the campfire, lightly snoring.

Istavan licked his lips again, and, keeping an eye on the others, he slowly crawled toward the cover of the rocks—when a small hand grabbed his jerkin!

"Ick!" Istavan had to stop himself from yelling out loud. "Phew, it's only the monkey girl. Be quiet, what are you so angry about? They're coming! Yeah, I know, I have a plan! No, I'm not running away. Damn meddlesome monkey!"

Istavan snatched up the girl and held his hand over her mouth. He began to run. Eastwards.

Meanwhile, in the west, back toward the Kes River, dust began to rise from the wasteland plain. The dust cloud came closer, the knights gradually becoming visible in its midst. First they seemed no larger than grains of sand, then they were pebbles, then rocks, until at last four hundred and fifty red knights and sixty white could be seen clearly through the cloud of dust.

Guin woke with a start. Seeing the riders bearing down on them, crossbows clenched in their gauntleted fists, he roared.

"What is it?" The twins stirred sleepily, rubbing their eyes.

For a second, Guin considered picking them up and running, but they were already in firing range, and there were at least five hundred of the mounted men. The leopard-man growled, a low rumble in his throat, and stood still.

"The mercenary's gone! And Suni, too!" he said.

"He betrayed us!" cried Remus.

Guin drew the twins to his side and stood fast in the dust and sand that now came swirling around them.

Five hundred crossbows and swords surrounded them on three sides. A sharp voice called for them to drop their weapons, and Guin complied.

They were captives of Gohra again.

Chapter Three

THE GENERAL'S PAVILION

—— I ——

The Marches sun rose high in the vault of the sky, its hard white light scorching the rocks of the Nospherus wildlands as if it meant to parch all things to dust.

In the shade of a jagged crag of sharp pale stone sat a wide tent of heavy cloth reinforced with leather—the pavilion of the Mongauli archduke's daughter, Amnelis. This was the center of a temporary base of operations for the Gohran knights that had crossed the Kes the night before.

From the spike at the pavilion's top flew the black lion of Gohra and the golden scorpion of Mongaul. In their fluttering shadow two pages stood, guarding the entrance. The rest of the Mongauli host, five hundred strong, stood at ease with their horses beside them, arrayed in concentric circles around the pavilion. They were at ease but alert, waiting for the signal to ride.

Guin, Rinda, and Remus sat on the bare ground under the watchful eyes of several knights. The sun seared their skin, especially that of Guin, whose burns ached and festered in the heat.

The three companions had not been bound or fettered, but still Rinda complained of their treatment to any knight who would listen. The only answer she ever received was a reiterated order to wait in silence. It seemed that Amnelis was preparing to question her captives here in the wildlands, without first returning to the temporary fortification on the river.

"Well, if we must wait, how about giving us some water, at least? How much longer do you intend to have us sit here in the dust? Some knights you are!"

Guin's injury, Istavan's desertion, and worry over what happened to poor little Suni—the weight of disaster was almost more than Rinda could bear. Yet no matter how much she pleaded with the knights, the answer was always the same, cold "Wait."

"Curse Jarn a thousand times for granting Mongaul any kind of victory at all. Even if your reign shall be very, very short lived!" shouted Rinda, but even that failed to evoke a response from the stolid guards.

At last a sharp order came from the tent: "Bring in the captives!"

Guards dragged the three companions to their feet. Rinda scowled at the one who pushed her toward the entrance, but in truth she was glad to be finally getting out of the blazing heat.

The sudden darkness of the pavilion interior rendered Rinda nearly sightless. Remus was quick to catch her when she tripped on something and nearly fell headlong onto the sandy floor.

As they entered they heard a female voice exclaim in surprise: "Are there only three?" It was the voice of a woman well accustomed to having her questions answered and her orders followed. "Vlon! Lindrot! Have a small squad of knights search the area at once. There were two others on that raft, and I want them found."

The two noblemen nodded and moved to give the orders. But after a moment's hesitation the speaker—Amnelis—stopped them. "On second thought, we already seem to have gotten the ones I was most interested in. Send out the squad, but there is no need for them to stray far from the main forces. Tell them to find any who are near, but to withdraw immediately at any sign of danger."

"As you command." Vlon made a crisp bow.

The captives, their eyes finally accustomed to the gloom inside the pavilion, lifted their drooping heads and looked around. The first thing that Rinda was able to make out in the darkness was a long white cloak that framed a gleaming figure.

Rinda blinked. The woman had long legs clad in tall, comfortable-looking white leather boots with cuffs adorned with silver inlay. The boots were protected with greaves of white metal, and they fit the legs of their wearer like sheaths around swords. Above the greaves and thigh-mail, the white armor flowed into a breastplate molded to a slender shape which proclaimed that, man or woman, the wearer was gifted with a graceful form that could catch many eyes and stir as many hearts. On the breast was a beautiful rendering of the Mongauli crest, generously set with gold and precious gems. And above that...

Rinda heard her brother gasp beside her. Above the armor, snowy white and purest gold mingled their brightness like a beacon in the dim light, more beautiful than the fabled yellow ore of Alceis.

Amnelis sat before them, her hands in white chainmail gauntlets resting idly on the arms of her chair. Her helm was off and the hood of her cloak was pulled back to let her unbound hair flow freely around the delicate features of her face. On her forehead she wore a thin band of silver set with a single glittering diamond. The twins were dazzled. She was a shining statue, molded by some unearthly artisan, incandescent against the dark background of the pavilion. So elegant was she, and so beautiful were her features, that the twins hardly noticed the knights standing to either side of her like servants attending a demigoddess.

Remus stood stunned, staring. Even Guin seemed smitten. Although his leopard mask revealed no emotion, there was a spark of something akin to admiration shining in his mysterious yellow eyes.

The proud little princess of Parros shrank back. It occurred to her quite suddenly that since the battle in the crystal city she had not had a proper bath and that her clothes were caked with mud, sand, and worse...not to mention the beaten leather boots and jerkin she wore, which looked like they might have been stolen from some poor stable boy. Her platinum-blonde hair was tangled beyond hope of ever getting a comb to run through it. And were her arms and legs not covered with scratches and scars? It seemed she had been a fugitive for so long, she would soon forget what it was to be royalty.

"So these are the twins of Parros." Amnelis's spellbindingly clear voice sounded like the peal of a bell in the soft quiet of the pavilion.

Remus, seeing his sister shrinking away, stammered, "Y-yes, ma'am. And you might be...?"

"Ma'am," Remus? Rinda thought. *If you're going to speak to the leader of the enemy at all, at least use the proper form of address!*

The response came in a voice that was soft but commanding. "I am Amnelis, General of the Right, daughter and proxy to Archduke Vlad of Mongaul, and captain of our white knights."

It was a bolt of lightning. *The white knights were there at the fall of the crystal city! Together with the black they brought our spires to the ground...they killed my lord father and lady mother!* Rinda closed her eyes and in the darkness beneath her eyelids she saw the black knights riding out from the rising smoke, and behind them the white knights, like horrid ghosts in their flowing white cloaks, cutting down the loyal and courageous of Parros.

"W-What does the Lady Amnelis want with us?" asked Remus, trying to sound brave though all he could think of was how imposing this woman was, and how he would never be as commanding as she.

He did not know that Amnelis, too, was rather out of sorts. As powerless as they looked, the bedraggled twins in their dirty leather garments had eyes that shone like stars. She could well see why they were called the "Pearls of Parros." And the leopard-headed warrior that had been captured with them....

Amnelis's deep green eyes shone with wonderment. She leaned forward, and the fascination in her gaze was plain to see.

Only her famed self-control kept her from gaping like a child at a magicker's show.

Gripping the arm of her chair, she muttered in a low voice, "What do we have here?"

Amnelis had seen warriors aplenty, though perhaps none as well muscled as Guin, whose build would have stirred envy in any man of the sword. She had, it was true, never seen one with a leopard head, but it was not this admittedly bizarre feature that sent a wave of unease through her. It was the eyes within the mask, yellow and bottomless, revealing nothing, the eyes of a cool predator. There was something about those eyes that she could not put a name to, something that made her swallow and set her heart beating faster.

To a duller, more superficial observer, those eyes might have seemed filled with simple violence—a wild, animal desire to kill, the kind of gaze that triggers a primitive response to run. But to those with the ability to see the true nature of things, such as Amnelis and Rinda, Guin's eyes held an unspeakable power, as terrifying to Amnelis as it was comforting to Rinda. To have called the force that burned in his eyes "ambition" would have been to understate it a thousandfold, to simplify its terrible complexity; it was a force that could change the world, a force vast and unnamable, yet not impersonal, a single-minded, unquenchable spirit that accepted no limits but those of its own—immense—strength.

Amnelis had a word for the life-energy that flowed from Guin's eyes and radiated from his powerful body, the energy that set him apart from all around him as only something intrinsically noble could: it was *destiny*. Here was the physical embodiment of a great, stormy destiny, made manifest in a half-beast, or half-god, form. A fierce, chaotic destiny that could change everything including the warrior it held in its grasp.

Amnelis's slender hand gripped the chair arm even tighter as she tried in vain to stop the trembling in her body. She swallowed again, this time noticing the perplexed look in the eyes of the captains around her—Lindrot and Vlon of the white, Melem and Kayn of the red—who rarely saw the general speechless. She had to begin the interrogation. She swallowed again.

"You." Her voice had fallen from the lilting alto with which she had addressed the twins to a gravelly rasp. "Who are you?"

Guin calmly met her gaze.

"I am Guin."

"Guin?"

"Yes."

"That…is your name?"

"Yes…I think."

"You think?"

Guin twitched his head like a lion trying to brush away a pesky fly, and spoke no further.

"You will answer the Lady's question!" barked Captain Vlon, but Amnelis raised her hand to silence him. She was slowly coming out of the trance into which those yellow eyes had sent her.

"Explain your…unusual appearance."

"I cannot."

"Then you were born like that? Or you were cursed by some magic?"

"I do not know. I have been thus as long as I can remember, which is not long." Guin fixed his yellow eyes on hers. "Can one not *be* if one cannot explain why?"

"Where are you from?"

"I do not know."

"Why you—" Vlon made a sign with his eyes at the knight standing guard behind the captives and stepped closer to the leopard warrior, impatient to regain control of the situation. "If you do not answer willingly, I will be happy to pry the answers from you! We are not like the weak knights of Parros, who are strangers to the proper use of pain!"

"Guin can't remember anything that happened to him before he woke up in the Roodwood! It's true!" Rinda burst out, unable to contain herself. "How can he tell you what he doesn't know?"

Amnelis's green eyes looked Rinda up and down disapprovingly, as if to ask what place the little girl had to speak out unbidden during her interrogation.

Rinda's voice trailed off, the words growing smaller in her mouth, until she shrank back into silence. Yet, the rage inside her was growing.

"Is this true? You have lost your memory?" Amnelis's gaze swung back to the leopard warrior.

Guin nodded slowly, as though he carried a great weight in his mind. "Try as I might, I can remember nothing."

"There are ways of making people remember that which

125

they have forgotten." Amnelis turned to the diviner who hovered like a specter in the gloom behind her. "Gajus!"

"My Lady."

"Bring your sphere and your board here, and look into this man's soul."

"As you wish."

Rinda began to protest, but a single cold glare from Amnelis made her swallow her words and shrink back once again from the woman's strength. The captain of the white knights was perhaps only four years her senior, yet Rinda felt herself an infant, powerless and miserable before this harsh, gorgeous enemy for whom an intense hatred now burned in her breast.

"That which you try to conceal will now be revealed. I advise you to forego any pretenses at once," Amnelis warned. Guin stood perfectly still.

"Until Gajus is through with his divinations, I will take you for your word—that you know not who you are, and have no memory of your past. If this is so, then, let me ask you: Why run from Mongaul? Why take the twins of Parros as your allies?"

Guin did not answer. Amnelis asked again, and still he remained silent.

"Speak! You made a choice, that is clear! If you have no ties to Parros, why side with them? Are you sympathetic to their cause after all? Answer me!" Amnelis roared, her face twisting in indignation. In a blur of movement she stood up from her chair, and stomped on the ground with her white and silver boots.

"Why are you in league with the orphans of Parros!"

"You will answer the Lady Amnelis!"

Amnelis and the captain shouted at the same time, her question and his command clashing in the air under the low pavilion roof.

Guin's leopard head tilted slightly to one side. Then, much to the surprise of all, he began quietly to laugh.

"What's so funny?" Amnelis slammed her boot into the hard-packed ground again.

"You are, lady."

"What?!"

"Beautiful daughter of the Archduke, perhaps your milksop Gohran soldiers find you imposing. But spare a real warrior your antics, I say."

Remus's mouth gaped open.

Rinda's head jerked upward, her eyes shining under falling silver locks of hair.

Amnelis was speechless.

"Fiend! Do not dare insult our Lady!" Vlon and Lindrot stepped up from both sides, hands on sword-hilts.

But Amnelis regained enough composure to raise her hand and wave them back.

All the captains present appreciated anew the general's steel will. Only for an instant had rage and humiliation choked her. Now she pulled herself together and managed to form a wry smile on her pale lips.

"Perhaps you have some secret from which you hope to divert my attention by provoking me, Guin?" she sneered, her voice gone cold. "Fine. I will explore that matter in the dungeons under Alvon Keep slowly, on the torturing table, perhaps. But let me ask one question now. From the cliffs near Alvon, I saw you floating down the Kes, but I am sure you were not three in number then. What happened to the other two? One of them, certainly, wore the black armor of Stafolos, and another one, strangely enough, seemed like one of the Nospherus Sem."

"I know nothing," replied Guin.

Amnelis looked as though she would lose her temper again, but she quickly forced down her wrath.

"Gajus, are you done yet?"

"My Lady," came the diviner's melancholy reply, "the divining sphere has shown this man."

"And?"

"Well, if I may—"

"Be brief. I have no need for theatrics, Gajus."

"Ah, so."

Uneasy wrinkles of consternation creased Gajus's withered and ugly face. He raised his hands, dry as fallen leaves, and placed them atop the cool surface of the divination sphere, but quickly pulled them back as if he had been burnt.

"I placed the divination sphere atop the divination board," stammered Gajus, "and I performed the reading by speaking the correct runewords to obtain the true sight of things; however…" he paused for effect.

Amnelis awaited his conclusion in silence.

"What was shown in the water mirror was nothing but a single, giant leopard."

"A leopard?" Amnelis furrowed her brow. "What is that supposed to mean? I did not ask for symbols, Gajus! Dispense with your usual mincing of words, or I will have you punished."

"I am sorry, but a leopard is only a leopard. It has no other meaning," came Gajus's reluctant answer. "I must conclude that this man's soul is that of a giant leopard. All else is vexingly blank, a white void. It seems less that he has lost his memory than that he never had such a thing to begin with.... All earthly folk are born with the accumulated memories of their race, held within them underneath their conscious selves. Even had I scryed a newborn infant, the waterboard would have shown more than it has for him! The board sees through any mask, my Lady, yet his true face is hidden still! I cannot see it...I cannot." Gajus fell silent.

Amnelis waited yet.

"This is my first experience with a being so unknowable," the wizened diviner added at last, looking as though he had suddenly aged another hundred years.

"Fool!" Amnelis spat out. She narrowed her eyes and dismissed the runecaster with a wave of her hand and a "You may go."

Then, sounding intensely irritated, she said, "Very well, let us say that this man is in fact a giant leopard that was set loose in Gohra. Perhaps the hands of some power from beyond the bounds of our knowledge and civilization set him down. Perhaps we behold nothing more than the unclean magic of Nospherus. If the demon Doal that rules Nospherus wishes to toy with us, there is a simple solution. Vlon!"

"My Lady!"

"Lindrot!"

"Here!"

"Give the order to return home. We will leave as soon as the searching party returns. Send a swift horse to Alvon to prepare them for our arrival. And these captives..."

A look of gratification tinged with cruelty crept across Amnelis's icy features as she gazed at her uncooperative captives. Gradually, a derisive smile came to her cool, shining lips.

"They will not need mounts. Tie their hands and feet with leather straps, and let them be dragged along the ground behind the rearmost horses. If this one is truly a beast-man, it suits him well."

Lindrot paused, glancing furtively over at the twins and their slender arms and legs.

Before he even had time to reply, Guin spoke in a voice approaching a roar. "The treatment I receive matters nothing to me, but let the children ride. One horse will suffice. They are young and exhausted. And they are highborn—the last remaining heirs of the holy royal line of Aldross. I am sure that conceding these barest of kindnesses would do no discredit to Gohra."

"General..." began Lindrot, looking up at Amnelis. Her face stiffened.

"Silence! You would have the Lady of Mongaul give the same order twice?"

"N-No, my Lady."

"Lady?" roared Guin. "You call yourself 'Lady'? Then you would at least give the children water and food. They are ready to collapse."

But then Guin felt a small, cold hand touch his arm, and he turned to look, his yellow eyes narrowing.

"As the princess of Parros, Rinda Farseer, I say to you: withdraw your request." Rinda's voice was uncannily calm.

Everyone stared, a strange feeling churning their stomachs, at the frail little girl sitting on the floor like a slave that had been dragged in for punishment.

Despite extreme fatigue, she kept her back straight as a rod and held her head high and proud. With a steady gaze she fixed the dazzling general. Anger, and unbendable royal pride, had released the fire that was her birth heritage into her veins. Her eyes shone like stars. She bit her lip, and her cheeks flushed bright.

Then a smile rose on her tense lips, the kind of smile that could not be sullied by the shame that had been laid upon her. She now remembered who she was. *I am the princess of Parros, the only girl child of the Holy Aldross the Third; I am Rinda Farseer, jewel of the Crystal Palace. Why, even the noblest of Mongauli are but descendants of my family's servants—or pretenders at that! Be proud, Princess Rinda, raise your head high. If you lower your head, so does Parros!*

Rinda felt the fear, the sinking inferiority, and the shame at being captured that had weighed within her dissipate entirely. In their place now was an imperishable, cold flame and a rage so powerful she dared not unleash it. She may not have realized it fully herself, but the dirty, mud-stained child that had been shoved into the pavilion had been replaced by a princess. Her willowy beauty was a slender moon to the radiance of the sun that was Amnelis, yet her youthful form shone with a white and silver that enraptured all the men in the pavilion, including Guin.

Amnelis, too, perceived the change in her adversary and was not pleased. The Lady of Mongaul's green eyes were severe, her lips taut. She made the air bristle with her cold fury—a mixture of vexation, disdain, and above all an urge to utterly dominate the waif-princess who had insolently challenged her queenship in the pavilion.

Amnelis glared at Rinda, and the princess of Parros returned her gaze without the slightest hint of fear. Rinda faced the one who had brought death to her mother and father, who had driven her and her brother from their kingdom home. This was the hated enemy who had given them nothing but hardship, an eternal enemy who could not be allowed to walk under the same sky.

Their eyes met, wild furious green and wrathful shining violet, and their gazes clashed almost audibly, striking sparks of pure emotion. It was a meeting of goddesses, each a proud mistress of her own domain. This, then, was the first time that the seer-princess of Parros and the warrior-lady of Mongaul stared each other down as sworn enemies—as captive and captor, as one whose father had been slain and one who had done the slaying. But there was more than this enmity between them, though it was likely they did not realize it. For in the moment their eyes met, there also flashed between them the mutual envy and hate of two beautiful women meeting for the first time; each found in the wholly different beauty of the other a deadly challenge to her own perfection.

Amnelis looked disapprovingly at the captive princess. Rinda's murderous gaze was unflinching. Amnelis's well-formed lips curled.

"My Lady, the red squad has just returned."

The flap covering the entrance to the pavilion lifted, diffusing the tension none of the men inside the tent could or would, and the unsuspecting red knight decorated with the plume-insignia of a squad captain came in to deliver his report.

"My apologies, General, the fugitives were not—"

"Very well!" Amnelis replied before he had finished. She suddenly rapped her gauntlets on her armored thighs, then swept back her heavy locks of hair. Her voice rang out high and clear.

"Give the order to march!"

The knights behind her, the diviner and messengers, all rose to their feet at once. Amnelis stalked back to the camp table to pick up her helm, then moved towards the exit. Passing Guin, she pointedly ignored him, as though she feared what would come should she acknowledge her burning fascination for the leopard-headed warrior. But as she passed Rinda, she paused, ostentatiously waving her rich golden hair, and cast a cold look downwards.

She was a head taller than the young girl. Where it was not covered by her fair armor, Amnelis's nearly mature skin—the general was only eighteen—glowed a milky hue tinted with rose.

She carried with her an aura of utter confidence in her beauty and her power, and in her knowledge of the effect they had on men and women alike.

Rinda lifted her head, unyielding, and though she was no runt, now face-to-face with Amnelis it was emphatically clear she was the less stately of the two. Rinda's violet eyes smoldered with rage.

Amnelis sneered.

"Wretched orphan."

The lady-general walked out of the pavilion without looking back. Her knights followed.

Rinda bit her lip so hard she nearly drew blood. Remus cast a worried look in her direction, but she did not notice. He did not know what she was feeling. He did not know she had decided to hate the Lady Amnelis of Mongaul for the rest of her living days.

— 2 —

The Mongauli knights were ready to march back towards the River Kes and Alvon Keep.

The children and the leopard-man were tied with leather straps tightly bound about their wrists and around their waists; the straps were fastened to the saddles of mounted knights. The captives walked between the two squads of white knights, who were in turn surrounded by rows of knights in red.

"Rinda...my wrists hurt," whimpered Remus, looking as though he might burst into tears at any moment.

His sister had not resisted when their captors tied on the leather straps. She had thrust her exquisitely slender arms out before her, as if to command that they be bound.

Now her face was stern. "Remus, your lord father died at the hands of these white knights. Always remember that! And you must remember how the Lady Amnelis preened in her arrogance, flushed with her wretched victory, and how she treated us, the prince and princess of Parros, like dogs! Should we be so lucky as to live, and should the day come that our father's kingdom rises once more, the first thing you must do as king is to wipe vile Mongaul—no, all of Gohra—off the face of the earth."

Remus looked at his sister, his eyes full of fear. "Is she going to kill us?"

"I would surely do so, were I the Lady of Mongaul!" Rinda declared, beyond trying to comfort her brother. "Remus, if we must die, we must die together. Please don't forget you're the heir of Parros! Be proud until the killing blade falls, and die with your head held high. Do you understand?"

Remus shook his head, his eyes filling with tears. Rinda's admonition stung him as badly as the pain from his tightly bound wrists.

"I don't want to die," Remus moaned, knowing full well how the admission of fear would anger his sister.

"Remus—" she began, when a rough grumble from Guin, bound with far sturdier cords than the twins, cut her off.

"Little Princess, not everyone is born as straight and true as you, or with as noble a heart." The leopard-headed warrior spoke solemnly. "You must not censure a soul different than your own, even should that soul wear a face like yours, for it was through no effort of your own that you were born as you are.

"And, Prince Remus, you must not be ashamed of who you are. There are not many heirs of kings who can so readily and honestly admit that they are afraid to die. You are no common boy."

"You're making fun of me."

Guin shook his head. "I'm saying you should be proud of who you are, little one."

"March!"

The order was passed from man to man down the long lines

in front of them. Slowly the five hundred knights began to move. The three captives suddenly found themselves yanked forwards by the taut straps around their wrists, and they had to step forward quickly to keep up.

The sun had risen high into the vast sky. From its heavenly vantage point it sent its rays to scorch all earthly things as it slowly slid westward.

"Guin," Rinda panted.

"Do not talk. You'll only tire more quickly."

"Guin, where could he have gone to, that—"

"Quiet!" hissed Guin.

The sound caught the attention of one of the knights riding in front of them, who turned to shout at them. "Talk while you can, leopard-freak. It'll only be a half-*twist* before those orphans of yours get so tired they'll fall down to be dragged along the ground by their pathetic wrists."

"Mongauli demon!" Rinda cursed in a hoarse voice, tears welling in her eyes. Guin waited, head down, until the knight lost interest and faced back forward.

When he was sure that he would not be heard over the plodding sound of their advance, nor, amidst the dust rising from five hundred horses' hooves, be seen talking, Guin spoke again in a low voice. "Do not say his name. He may be our only lifeline now."

"What? That scoundrel's probably so happy with his little bit of treachery he's off sleeping peacefully under some rock."

"We do not know that. And even if he were, we have no grounds to accuse him. He's a mercenary, and we certainly never paid him. All that's left for us to do is to trust Jarn and his crippled son, Hope."

Istavan had not been sleeping; nor indeed had he abandoned his chance companions as Rinda suspected, though it was true that he felt no particular loyalty to them, nor any responsibility to alter their predicament. No, the veils of emotion and honor could do little to cloud the eyes of the Crimson Mercenary, as keen as they were for the gleam of profit.

Yet, circumstances prevented him from enjoying his perfect evasion of the Mongauli forces as much as he would have liked. He was, after all, stuck in the no-man's-land of Nospherus, a place filled with Doal-knows-what dangers, and no matter how skilled he was with the sword, one man on foot didn't have much of a chance of surviving more than a day or two out here alone. Now, if he were a superhuman warrior like Guin, maybe...but that was not the case.

Nor had he any special knowledge of Nospherus or its denizens. Few folk did who had been raised in the Middle Country. Just thinking about the yidoh that had engulfed his leg or the bigmouths that roamed both water and land set the hairs on the back of his neck bristling. It was scant consolation that he was unlikely to be threatened by water creatures any time soon, since he didn't even have a raft with which to make the crossing back to Gohran lands.

This is not good, not good. Not good at all. By the hundred drooping ears of Jarn up in heaven, I must admit I'm in a bit of a fix.

Things had gone quite well that morning, considering. He

had seen the dust from the approaching riders, abandoned his look-out duties, and made a clean escape, except for his having to drag off the protesting Sem girl to keep her from giving him away. Istavan Spellsword had a special talent for saving his own skin. The mercenary could be faulted for failings of many kinds, but this gift of his was certainly as exceptional as Guin's superhuman strength and willpower. Istavan knew when a situation was turning sour; often he could read the signs of trouble hours before it came. His hunches were pure gold.

This morning, for example. He thought back on the events that had begun the day...

Crouching behind an outcrop, Istavan had watched the knights sweep over his companions' camp. He was quite sure that, while the capture of Guin and the twins would satisfy the Mongauli band to some extent, they would undertake at least a cursory search for him and Suni. So he had dragged off the Sem, who shrieked in her incomprehensible monkey language, and had hidden in the broken land. Then, instead of doing the obvious and heading east to put distance between them and the search parties, he had gone around behind the advancing knights.

Now, safely ensconced atop a rugged cliff, he lazily watched the searchers when, as expected, they headed off to the east. A temporary encampment had been set up beneath the cliff, with a large military pavilion and horses and knights resting in the shade. Istavan surveyed the scene and chuckled deep in his throat.

"Hey, you, monkey-girl! I know you don't understand me,

but I'll tell you something good anyway. The finest ditch-wis-
dom. Want to know the best way to hide? Get as close as you can
to whoever's looking for you, and wherever they go, you follow
them! Follow the followers, get it? No, I see you don't. What it
means is that we can sit up here and enjoy the sun in relative
safety, that's what it means."

Istavan looked up at the sky and swore lightly.

"But maybe that isn't such a good idea after all, eh? Ach, it's
like we're in that tale where the frost spirit Laala wanders onto
Ruah Sungod's bronze disc and melts in half a *twist*—though I
doubt it'll take us that long! And to top it off I'm bloody hungry.
Huh? What's that? Got something to say?"

Istavan twisted his handsome features into a scowl and
roused himself from his comfortable perch to glare at the ape-
girl, who had suddenly started up a ferocious twittering. She
pulled on the mercenary's hand, showing every sign of over-
whelming anxiety.

Lacking anything better to do, Istavan let the girl's animated
gestures lead his gaze down to the bottom of the cliff. There was
something going on down there. He frowned. From this distance, the figures looked no bigger than beans in the sand, but
Istavan could clearly make out the shapes of Guin and the twins
of Parros in front of the great pavilion that clearly belonged to
whomever was commanding the force of knights.

The mercenary of Valachia couldn't understand a word that
Suni said, but her intent was clear from her tone and gestures.
She grew increasingly agitated, pounding her furry feet on the
rock, pointing down towards the pavilion, making pleading

gestures to Istavan and tugging on the sword in the sheath at his waist. Her chestnut eyes flared with a fierce, determined light as she clung to him, begging him to save Rinda.

"Aluura, iminitto, grah!"

Istavan scowled. The girl's words were gibberish but she was certainly saying something like "cowardly cretin," or he was no mercenary.

"Fool monkey! Keep squawking like that and I'll stick a spit through you and cook you for dinner," he threatened, and put up a finger over his lips in a universal gesture. But Suni seemed so intent on her mission that, if she understood him, she did not show it. Instead she tugged even harder on his scabbard, her round eyes accusing the runaway mercenary.

"Get your stinking monkey hands off me!" Istavan hissed, tired of her insistent whines. "What's your problem, anyway? Them? Leave those fools be. Look, that Guin can handle anything Jarn Fateweaver throws at him. If he can handle slime-creatures, he can handle a few knights, okay? Let them deal with their own problems. You should be more worried about saving yourself. Isn't that the way of your land? Aaaah, shut up!"

Istavan's obsidian eyes, flashing with exasperation, narrowed. His hand flew to his side, as if he were about to draw the sword at his waist and cut the girl in two. Suni's high-pitched chattering stopped abruptly and she hopped back with a shriek.

Quickly the little Sem scampered out of the range of Istavan's blade, warily watching his every move. Seeing her eyes round with fear, the ill-mannered mercenary was unable to contain his laughter.

"I see you've finally got it through your monkey head that I mean business. Be very afraid, monkey-girl!" Istavan growled in mock ferocity, clutching his sides to stifle his laughter. Seeing that his merriment angered Suni made him laugh harder. The young mercenary still had moments when he behaved more like a willful, mischievous boy than a man nearing the age of twenty, a trait that had angered a good share of people in recent years, though Istavan himself would have been the last to care.

But Suni's desperate determination was unabated, for Rinda had saved her life, and in return, Suni had given Rinda her heart. She cared more for the girl with platinum-blonde hair than perhaps Rinda cared for herself. Now the princess was in danger, and Suni could think of nothing else.

The mercenary chuckled as Suni glared at him with untrusting eyes. He was pleased to see that she had abandoned any hope of getting him to help; at least, she was not accosting him and tugging on his sword anymore. Instead she fell deep in thought, until suddenly, she sprang to her feet with the speed of a wild animal.

In a flash the girl was scampering down the rocky slope with the nimble expertise of a true child of the wasteland.

"Whoa, hey! Monkey!" By the time the startled Istavan was able to jump forth, she was already sliding off the edge. "Hey, stop! Where do you think you're going, monkey! Hey!" Istavan reached for her pointlessly; Suni was already far beyond his grasp. The little Sem girl flashed one glance back at him with her chestnut-brown eyes, then scampered off on her tiny feet, never looking back again.

"Aah..." Istavan's cursing died into a sigh as he watched her go. The little hairy shape leapt in rapid zigzags down the opposite side of the cliff whereon Istavan had made his temporary hideout.

The Crimson Mercenary sat for a while, watching her go. Finally he spat. "What was that all about? Damn monkey..." A sudden rush of anger overtook him and he leapt to his feet. He yelled at the spot where Suni had been hiding, "What's the big idea, glaring at me like that! By the three-and-a-half curls of Jarn's tail, I haven't done anything wrong!"

His youthful face twisted in a dramatic scowl. He stared towards the cliff base. After a moment's hesitation, during which he repeated to himself that it was not his problem, he lay down on the hard ground again, with exaggerated indifference—then just as soon leapt up to his feet.

"They got themselves into it!" Istavan grumbled to no one in particular. "That leopard-head is master of his own fate, anyway. I'm not doing so well, am I, running fugitive like this. Maybe I should have sold the twins to the Gohrans early on—worked out a deal. Might've even scored rank among the knights. Come to think of it, I *was* sort of curious how the archdukes' power struggle would play out after the Mongauli conquest of Parros..."

The mercenary thoughtfully scratched at the bristle on his chin. He knew he needed a plan, but what? Spellsword or no, he couldn't imagine making it across the badlands all by himself. Yet the prospect of taking on five hundred elite troops wasn't too tempting either. And he certainly didn't owe those fugitives enough to risk his own skin. They hadn't even hired him, so he could hardly feel obligated....

"Huh?" Istavan suddenly broke out of his reverie and squinted down through the blazing sunlight.

There was a commotion below among the knights. Apparently orders to march had been given. In unison, the knights rose up from their rest, stowing canteens and rations in their packs, strapping on chaps and gloves, and bringing their horses into formation. Quickly they closed ranks, the captains riding back and forth among them.

The mercenary cautiously slipped along the rocks until he found a vantage point where he would not easily be seen, and he flattened himself on the ground at the cliff's edge.

A small cloud of dust approached from the east and turned into the search party that had been sent out to look for Istavan and Suni. The searchers joined the other knights to complete the formation, which from above looked like a white stamen surrounded by red petals. At the head of each rank, drummers rapped a quick beat on their drumskins, and the barren rocks of Nospherus echoed back. It was the signal to depart.

At last, a small group emerged from the pavilion. From atop the cliff, Guin's tall, heroic form and tawny leopard head were the easiest to pick out, though Istavan's sharp eyes could easily see the platinum-blonde twins as well, one to either side of the warrior. In the rising dust, they were like exotic flowers that had sprung inexplicably from the dry desert rock.

The knights pushed them out and made them kneel, then

with leather straps bound their waists and outstretched hands. Istävan watched unblinking as the captives were led to the middle of the formation and tied to horses.

Then, something else near the pavilion, which was being dismantled, caught his eye: a figure proudly mounting a white horse that stood ready.

Istavan swallowed.

He could not see the commander clearly at such a distance, but he felt something when he looked upon the form. He scowled, and closed his eyes, deep in furious thought. Then he sprang to his feet and nodded to himself, with the air of someone who has made an important decision.

Istavan was ready for action.

$$3$$

"Guin..."

Five hundred knights advanced in somber silence through the wildlands of Nospherus.

Captain Melem, an illustrious warrior of Gohra, led the vanguard, at the head of the Third Troop of the Fifth Red Knights. Captain Kayn's Second Troop rode behind him, ranks divided to leave riding-space for the two squads of white knights led by Lindrot and Vlon. Behind them rode the pride of Alvon, the one-hundred and fifty knights of Astrias's First Troop, acting as rear guard for the host.

Amnelis, the Lady of Mongaul, rode at the heart of the formation, outshining all others in her splendid raiment, her aura of command effortlessly extending to direct the five hundred elite soldiers who surrounded and guarded her.

She had removed her helm, and the sparkling of the white steel of her armor mingled with the golden rush of her long hair, both shining in the light of the afternoon sun that had now begun to slant towards the Marches horizon. Even the hot sandy wind that whipped the dry dirt of Nospherus—the fierce wind that the knights called "Doal's Breath," which covered them in sand and drove the dust into every chink of their mail—seemed to part and make way for her.

"Guin...Oh...Guin!" Towards the rear of the proud Gohran ranks the last scions of the royal line of Parros staggered along, bound like slaves or animals being brought to market, tugged by indifferent horses and prodded by callous knights who rode close after them. The lead-ropes chafed at the skin of their wrists until their clothes were stained red with blood.

"Guin...I can't go any further..." Rinda's voice was so hoarse it was hardly recognizable as hers.

"Rinda, be strong..." Remus murmured weakly, trying to encourage his sister, but his weary knees buckled with every step.

"What's wrong, you two? I didn't expect the Pearls of Parros to give up so easily," whispered Guin, not unkindly. Rinda lifted her eyes and looked at him through a haze of fatigue. He strode stoically behind the horses, head held high, showing not a sign of weariness; when their gazes met it seemed as though some of his incredible, wild energy poured into her, and she was able to walk for a while without stumbling.

"Remus," Rinda said falteringly, "Remus, remember this fatigue, this shame. May the burden of our lord parents' deaths, and the curse of the people of Parros, and all of our own pain come to pass unto our foes."

"Don't talk. Save your strength," scolded Guin.

Rinda laughed hoarsely. "Somehow, it seems easier when I talk. Oh, Guin! Why did this have to be? Only a week ago we were living in peace in the Crystal Palace...it all changed so suddenly."

For all her bravery and strength of spirit, Rinda was still a child of fourteen. She moaned softly, a half-cry through lips dried and cracked by the windborne sand. For a whole day she had not had a sip of water, and her throat was parched. Her eyes were dry, too; the tears she had held back had run from the pores of her skin as sweat and evaporated into the desert air.

"We cannot know Jarn's design. My loss of memory, not even knowing how I came to be who I am, and now this trial that we face—all of these things are part of some grand scheme that only he understands."

"Oh, Guin—I need water," Remus moaned. One of the red knights riding ahead of them turned in his saddle to glance at the boy. These were the red knights of Gohra, formidable and feared, but it was not true that all of them were demons. They were loyal to Amnelis, and so none thought to defy her orders, as cruel as they were. Still, though they had dragged many prisoners behind them, those had been strong fighting men like the leopard-headed warrior. Seeing the two children of Parros stumbling along in the dust was a sight too painful for many of them.

"Don't speak of water," Guin rasped. "It will only make it worse."

"But...but Guin...I can't walk anymore."

"Remus, be strong." Now it was Rinda's turn to encourage her brother. "Guin?"

"Yes, child?"

"I was thinking, this sand and these rocks, they seem so very hot—and as we walk, my leg are starting to shake...but...is it just the heat?"

"No. I had noticed it myself," Guin replied. "Can you sense it? There's some kind of ill humor in the air, thick and cloying, almost alive—as though one of those jelly-creatures were riding the wind, getting into my throat and itching me...."

"I wonder if the Mongauli have noticed?"

"No talking!" one of the knights riding ahead of them hollered. Then he added in a lower voice, "You'll only collapse faster, understand?"

The knight had spoken kindly, but hearing her enemy speak was more than Rinda's noble heart could bear. Every muscle in her body tensed, and she licked her lips and searched for the right words to spit back at him.

Just then, however, there was a commotion towards the front of the host, and for the first time the ranks broke their tight formation.

"Bigeater!"

"In the sand!"

The cry went up from the front lines, followed by the panicked whinnying of horses and the shouting of riders trying to calm their mounts. The air was filled with the shouts of captains bellowing orders, trying to maintain control.

Bigeaters, though denizens of dry land, were closely related to the bigmouths that prowled the Kes. In shape they were much the same as the bigmouths—eerily animated sets of giant jaws filled with sharp teeth—but instead of cruising the dark waters, they lurked in depths of sand. They also tended to be much larger in size.

Without warning, a bigeater had come speeding from some hidden lair, danced up through the dunes and lunged at a young knight in the Melem Troop as he sat upon his horse.

With its first bite, the monster tore the horse in half. The rider was thrown, and fell tumbling and screaming into the hole in the sand from which the bigeater had sprung. Then the fiend ate the horse as though it were a gati grain ball while the fallen knight tried frantically to clamber up the crumbling slope of sand.

"Aggyaaah!"

The young knight screamed suddenly, collapsing on his side in the sandy pit. Just when it seemed that he was about to reach solid ground, the pale white tentacle of some other creature in the pit had lashed up from below and wrapped around him. Slowly he was dragged back down into the darkness. Around the pit, his fellows covered their ears, sickened by his awful cries for help.

"Go, help him! Quickly!" the nearest captain shouted.

"It's no use!" one of the knights replied frantically. "A mouth-of-the-desert's got him!"

The men backed away from the pit, not wanting to see or hear their comrade's death throes. But just before the wretched victim disappeared into the collapsing hole, a few of them saw something at the base of that twisted, pallid tentacle that groped like the living root of some demon-tree: a blood-sucking mouth, belching horrid fumes into the air as it gaped to bite its prey.

There was no saving him—the third man to die since the

force had set out from Alvon. Averting their eyes and turning their backs upon the screaming, the knights set with a vengeance upon the bigeater that had just finished its meal of horse. This monster they could reach, and they stuck it through with spears and tore it to bony pieces on the sand. Then they poured oil into the pit of the mouth-of-the-desert and set it on fire.

The rocky ground was littered with blood and flesh and entrails. Nothing recognizable was left of the horse. The knights tossed the remains of the bigeater into the flaming pit, then drew away so as not to be caught by the flailing tentacles of the burning creature as it writhed in its tortured death throes. A few of the men gagged and retched, unable to contain their nausea at the stench of the mouth burning alive. So different were the cursed denizens of Nospherus from the gentle beasts of the Middle Country, so fearsome and so vile, both in life and in death.

Yet to venture into the wildlands with only five hundred men, and emerge with only three lost after a night and a day, would be close to a miracle.

Not bothering to erect a grave for their fallen comrade, or even to observe a moment of silence before the funeral pyre of burning flesh, the Gohran forces resumed their march at once. They knew that Count Ricard should have constructed a simple fort on the barren side of the Kes by now. Amnelis planned to get there with her three captives by nightfall.

Yet the need to match their pace to that of Guin and the two children, and the encounter with the bigeater and the mouth-of-the-desert, had slowed them down considerably, so that when they finally reached a place where they could look down on the dark sparkle of the Kes, the deep purple cloak of twilight had already fallen around them.

Perhaps it was a trick of the wind, but as darkness enveloped them, the angel hair that had been absent during the day appeared again and in ever increasing quantities. It seemed that the closer they came to the river, the thicker the angel hair became.

The sticky white strands, neither animal nor plant, adhered to their armor and their faces and then just as quickly melted into nothingness. For a while, the knights were able to brush most of it away, and they paid it little heed. Yet, as they proceeded, the angel hair grew thicker still, as though each thin strand were summoning all its brethren. Or perhaps it was that the mass of humans and horses, so rare in the wildlands of Nospherus, acted as a beacon to the angel hair, the living heat that the cavalry radiated stimulating in it some primal thirst for warmth. The drifting strands gathered silently, approaching from all directions until they surrounded the knights like a pale white cloud.

The captains gathered together as they rode and spoke briefly about the matter. It was known that angel hair was harmless, and the force seemed to be proceeding unimpeded through the cloud, so they gave the orders to continue on course. But then, one of the knights happened to gaze upwards...

"Look!" A shocked yell rang out across the ranks. Startled, the men looked up and gasped. The sky was gone. All they could see above them was angel hair!

The Nospherus gloaming had dimmed to dark purple, a color as ominous and oppressive as the clear violet of Rinda's eyes was pure and promising. So thick and dark were the heavens in Nospherus nearly every night that not a single star shone through. It was always as though a formless, night-colored creature, gelatinous and oozing, were spreading like a membrane to deprive earthly creatures of the comfort of a starry sky. But now, beneath the dreary canopy hung thousands of strands of angel hair!

Even to those who were sure that the strands were harmless, it was a disconcerting sight—one that made dauntless knights tremble. It seemed that Janos had sent a cloud to rain upon them alone, a cloud of white fibers, gathering silently like the thousand cilia of a swalloworm waiting in the deeps to envelop its prey. The entire sky appeared to be covered by the pale angel hair mist. The cloud hung low before the riders and behind them and to all sides, obscuring everything with a ghastly white imbued with the purple of the night beyond.

The Mongauli soldiers began to waver. They would face Sem armies or Cheironia's fearsome Dragon Knights and Lion Knights without hesitation, but something about the gently swaying pale-white wisps that descended silently upon them plunged their spirits and awakened primal fears that had lain dormant deep within them.

"Gajus!" Amnelis called for the runecaster, and a few of the men thought they heard in her voice the faintest trace of a trembling that not even she could entirely suppress. "What is this?

Tell me!"

The aged caster took up the knotted rune-forms of his prayer cords and with his weathered hands wordlessly groped their shapes in a way that was somehow irritating to all who watched him.

"Angel hair is harmless, so it wouldn't be...attacking us, would it?" the general inquired.

Gajus shook his head. "I have never heard word or story of such a thing, my Lady."

"You're a diviner. Divine!"

"Then, I would say that their gathering about is neither an omen for bad, nor for good..."

"Useless!" Amnelis snorted, ending her exchange with the old caster. Few of her troops had been near enough to overhear it, and even those who were nearby were too occupied with wiping away the angel hair that snowed down upon their faces to pay close attention to the old man's words.

Some of the knights had begun chatting to shake off the chill fear the angel hair had brought.

"Ever heard a tale like to this, Marus?"

"No, never. One o' my cousins is on one of those homesteads on the Marches. He's been living a long time in the woods near Tauride, and he talked about the angel hair out there. He said it was harmless stuff—creepy, but harmless. That was just before I got transferred to Alvon Keep, come to think of it...."

"Nah, you listen to me. There's nothing normal about this. I've got a feeling in my gut, I have. This bodes ill, brothers."

"Hold your words, Hendree."

"No, no, I've got a strong spirit-sense, you know."

"Yurik knows things, let's ask him. Hey, Yurik! Yurik! You ever heard of this happening? This normal?"

"I've heard of no such thing, but it seems to me that out here in Nospherus, anything's possible."

"Well, listen!" shouted a man who had been silent until then. "I've heard that this angel hair stuff is the spirits that slipped from the mouths of the dead!"

"That's nothing to be yelling, you!"

"By the face of Janos' merciful mother!"

"You know, when the crystal city fell, our Mongauli knights, black and white both, rode through the streets and cut down harmless city-folk from horseback."

"Yaaa! Silence your ill-omened tongue!"

The wind that had died down picked up again slightly, sending ripples through the silky envelope of angel hair that surrounded them. Someone lit a torch and thrust it towards the undulating cloud. Where the flame touched it long enough, the cloud quickly melted and vanished away into nothingness, leaving a window through which the deep purple of the starless night sky could be seen. But moments later, the surrounding strands would slide together to fill the gap, forming an even thicker layer of white.

The five hundred knights had gradually ceased to move forward. Though each strand of angel hair was harmless alone, the quantities that now fell upon their faces and mouths threatened to suffocate them and forced them to devote considerable attention to brushing them away. Furthermore, the impenetrable nature of the white clouds presented an even graver danger by restricting vision in all directions to only a few paces. Were the knights in the front ranks to recklessly continue onward, they might easily fall upon a mouth-of-the-desert with no one behind them any the wiser.

The three troop captains Melem, Kayn, and Astrias sped their horses to the middle of the formation and approached the general.

"Lady Amnelis, I must inform you that we cannot proceed in these conditions. It is too dangerous!"

"Our men are beginning to fear."

"We have come to the decision that camping here for the night presents the least danger to the well-being of our men."

Amnelis glanced aside at the captains of her personal guard. Vlon and Lindrot met her gaze and nodded.

"Very well," she said after a moment's consideration. "We have brought with us rations for three days, and there can only be three tads or so between us and the River Kes now. Better to make that trip in the daylight. Give the order to prepare camp. Under the circumstances..." Amnelis glanced up at the undulating white cloud, "we will tie the horses in a circle around us for defense, set up a triple-patrol on constant rotation, and light a large bonfire in the middle of camp. The men are not to take off their armor, even when resting. We leave at first sign of dawn, and we will be in Alvon Keep by the time the sun has risen to the arch of the sky."

The three captains nodded their assent and moved to give the orders. Amnelis called out to them as they turned to leave.

"Let us be ready lest, by some ill chance, this angel hair should indeed prove harmful. Order each of your men to carry a torch at his waist, and be prepared to light them at the watch fires. A little bit of flame can melt away these strands."

"As you command."

"Now, go!"

Amnelis watched the three captains hurry to their duties. Then she spoke again, more to herself than to the three who remained with her—the two captains of the white and Gajus Runecaster.

"Troubling, this. I had made up my mind to push through whatever may come to reach the fortification on the Kes by nightfall."

"The circumstances dictate another course of action," whispered the caster.

"The angel hair weighs on my mind. Why have I never heard of this happening? What sort of change might have brought this about?"

"My Lady, this is Nospherus…" was Gajus's reply.

"Is that your excuse for not having a clue?" Amnelis snapped. But then she bit her rose-colored lip and looked up at the pallid demon-mists swirling above.

"I will raise the pavilion. You must rest, my Lady," a page said deferentially. But the lady-general showed no sign of dismounting.

The knights hurriedly prepared for a night in the Nospherus wildlands. A giant watchfire was lit, and the men mixed gati balls with water to make gruel for supper.

The straps were removed from the captives' wrists, and the three companions were each given a thin bedroll on which to lie behind the horses. They fell down upon their hard beds and for a while did not move. Their spirits had been drained to the point that it was all they could do just to keep breathing.

Amnelis for her part gave no orders regarding the captives. It was as though she had entirely forgotten about them. A few knights approached with canteens of water, grain balls, and oily salve for the cuts on their wrists.

Rinda and Remus drank deeply from the canteen, and for a while could think of nothing else. Even after long draughts of water, they did not touch the gati balls. Their throats were so dry from the day's march that they feared they would be unable to swallow the hard grains.

Guin took a single sip of water from the canteen, sloshed it back and forth upon his tongue, and spat it out into the sand. He then picked a piece of dried fruit out of one of the grain balls. After softening it in his hands, he put it in his mouth and slowly began to chew.

While Guin worked on restoring his strength, the twins collapsed on the ground and lay there, looking up at the shifting sky above them.

"It...it's really quite odd," Rinda said in a tiny voice. "The Mongauli soldiers fear the angel hair so much they've stopped, but I'm not afraid of it at all. It's strange, but I almost feel comforted...like I've seen this same thing happen a long, long time ago."

Remus nodded. "I'm not feeling scared either. It's even kind of beautiful. It's like the cloth of spider webs and dew that the maiden Ayin gives you when you die and go up to the halls of Janos."

"I feel like if it wrapped around me, I could fly, fly through the sky. Don't you, Remus? I wonder. Maybe angel hair *are* the spirits of the dead. Maybe these are the souls of all those thousands of people who died when Parros burned...."

Guin glanced warily at the twins, doubtful of their assessment of the angel hair, but he saw that their conversation seemed to be helping them calm down and rest. That was a good thing. He went on chewing bits of his grain ball silently.

The knights on watch had also heard the twins speak, but when they looked at the two children and at the white, living mist that hung above their heads, they were silent and only made the sign of Janos close to their breasts.

The wind had died down, but the angel hair continued to sway, its motion intensifying until it seemed like the knights and their prisoners were at the bottom of a pallid purple sea. The Nospherus night grew deeper, filling the Gohrans with unease. A stealthy, prickling fear began to creep among them—a fear that they would not see the sun rise again.

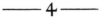

—— 4 ——

The night deepened.

The captains had spent many hours sitting in council in Amnelis's pavilion, but they had concluded their deliberations at last and each had returned to his respective command. Now, in the flickering torchlight within the pavilion, a page wetted towels with precious water and carefully cleaned the dust and sand of Nospherus from the general's weary limbs. When he had finished, he helped the lady into her bed of layered linens and snuffed the torch.

Outside, there were few who slept. They could not be at ease in a place like this as they could in the safety of Alvon Keep. Flames from the watchfires leapt towards the mantled sky. The men were kept busy feeding the flames with bits of wood and dried moss and whatever other fuel they had been able to gather or carry with them.

The soldiers ate, looking up at the angel hair uneasily all the while, and smacked their lips and thought longingly of the sweet mulsum honey-wine that they were forbidden to drink on the march. When the men exchanged glances they marveled at each other's faces, every last one of which was caked and discolored by the Nospherus sand. For them there was no water for washing.

When the knights lit the watchfires, the swarming canopy of angel hair grew thinner and thinner above the central flames until it took the shape of a vast hovering ring. The men half expected more of the white tendrils to swarm from the edges into the central void, to fill it, as before. To their relief, however, it appeared that no more of the peculiar strands were arriving. The knights' unease began to settle when they saw the power of their watchfires' flames, and they slowly grew accustomed to the shifting white mist hanging above their heads like a gentle, swaying creature looking down on them with expressionless eyes. The fire was bright and warm, and soon the morale of the knights had recovered enough that they felt ready to chat amongst themselves, albeit in whispers.

There were two main topics of conversation: the angel hair, and the freakish captive that they had dragged with them from the wildlands interior.

Every squad had a scholar, respected for his knowledge of the world's many mysteries, or perhaps a fellow renowned for his sixth sense and intuitive way of comprehending the unknown. These men now spoke thoughtfully to the other knights, their faces half lit by the fires.

"It's an ill omen for sure," one proclaimed. "If I'm wrong, may I eat the blade of my longsword, and throw in the scabbard!"

"What is?" whispered another of the knights. "The angel hair...or that freak?"

"Both of 'em!" replied the first man, taking a swig from his canteen. "If it were just one of 'em, I might be willing to blame it on chance. 'Anything can happen in Nospherus,' and all that. Aye, I'm sure there're plenty more freakish things out there in the night, my friend. But the leopard-headed man and this angel hair? Coming right after the bad turn at Stafolos—"

"Me mates Gulun and young Orro were at Stafolos when she fell," interrupted another knight. He had a thick accent and an eager voice and his face was ruddy in the firelight. "Someone just tell me if that monster had anything t' do with the fall o' the keep...or even if 'e was just the omen that brought in the bad luck. I'd like t' do a few things t' the man responsible for getting me mates made into corpses by those wildling Sem."

"Ah, let it rest—it'll do no good," a third man put in. "If you could cut fate with a sword, we'd have no need of magic!"

The scholar gave a hollow laugh. "You know what I think?" he said, looking around to make sure he had an attentive audience. "Now I don't want anyone spreading this. Fact is, it's not the sort of thing I would say out loud if I didn't trust each and every one of you. But I got a feeling that the Golden Scorpion Palace should never have laid its heavy hand on Parros."

The knights around him gasped, looks of shock on their faces.

"No, no, think on it. All these odd happenings, starting with the fall of Stafolos, have had something to do with the Pearls of Parros and that spawn of Cirenos that's guarding them."

"Hmm...now that you mention it..." one of the men nearby nodded thoughtfully.

"We call the wheel that Jarn spins *fate*," the scholar continued, "And the reed in his hand that guides his threads we call
coincidence. Only Jarn knows which thread will fall into his pattern and when. But these last few days—"

"I'll tell you which way the weave is headed," said one of the
knights gruffly. "I've got a thread here I call a *noose*, and once I
use it to string up those two pearls and their beast-nanny we'll
be rid of their curse for good!"

The knights laughed. Only the scholar seemed not to be
amused. "If you listen to what I'm saying, you'll see that it's not
our captives that are the source of this curse on Mongaul."

The laughter quieted down. More knights gathered around
the fire to listen. The scholar surveyed his audience with a satisfied look. He began to speak again as though he were giving a
lecture to students in an academy.

"The beautiful city of Crystal, topped by the Crystal Palace,
was a city of spells—spells, mind you!—and the dais of the shrine
of Janos. That kingdom was thousands of years old! Things
happened there that we Gohran newcomers could only see in
our wildest dreams. Well, you all know that, but I'll tell you
something you don't. There was another palace beneath the
Crystal Palace, called the Forbidden Temple. And since the days
of the ancients, casters and maidens have been enshrined there
to watch over the sacred remains of the High King Aldross—and
still lurk in there. Every king-to-be had to go down into the
Forbidden Temple to undergo a test—a meeting with the
mummy of the high king! We didn't give any thought to any of
that, but Parros is such a place!

"Wait, man. Are you saying that freakish things are happening to us because our archduke, ever ahead of Kumn and Yulania, went ahead and took the crystal city for Mongaul? Is the blood of Parros on our hands?"

"Yes! And what's more, if what's transpired so far is all that ever happens to us, I'd count us luck—"

The scholar's pronouncement changed abruptly to a yelp when a horsewhip cracked against his shoulder. He looked up to see Kayn, the troop leader, staring angrily down at him from horseback. Immediately the scholar threw himself prostrate on the ground.

"Spread confusion through the troops with your careless words, and you'll be fighting bigmouths in the Kes with your bare hands, soldier!" snarled the captain, his voice harsh with fury. "And the rest of you! Next time you hear any buffoon spouting groundless rumors like this, try stuffing grainballs in your ears. You'll be all the better for it!" Kayn glared all around him, then spurred his horse and trotted away from the watchfires.

The knights sat silently for a while, each lost in his own uneasy gloom. Then suddenly one of them shouted "Look!" and pointed up at the sky. The men looked up and gasped sharply in unison. While they had been talking, a gentle wind had picked up and blown away all traces of the white gauze-like curtain that had hung above them. Someone whistled in amazement. The sky was clear.

The milky white sea that had roiled above them had changed into a deep night sky, a vast high plain of ultramarine. For it also seemed that the night winds had blown away the unclean, almost sticky Nospherus air. Everything was somehow crisper and clearer. And the stars...

The knights stood transfixed, staring upwards. A starry sky was rare in Nospherus, where all too often the heavens were shaded with heavy clouds—jealous clouds that never rained on the parched earth. It was said that Doal would not grant passage to the starlight. But tonight the Marches sky was plain before them. The astrologers tell that the constellations in the sky are not permanent as most would believe, that their alignments have shifted and wandered dramatically from what they were in ancient times. But to the ordinary men of Gohra, who knew only one night sky, the one of their lifetimes, the familiar shapes that were visible in the heavens now were deeply comforting.

Some of the celestial lights shone fiercely while others, like the giant red star of the War God, gave off a duller light. But amongst all of the familiar stars, each with its own legends, there were two that stood out brightest of all. The first was called the White Bear by common men. It was the Pole Star: a beacon to sailors since ancient times, hanging like a lantern in the cold sky above the black humps of the Ashgarn Mountains in the north. Its sagacious light shone down on mortal men doomed to follow their brief fatal paths. It witnessed their deeds, passed judgment upon them, and mocked their simplicity even as they looked to it for direction.

The second great star hung over the ancient, storied mountains of Kanan that silently overlooked the wildlands from their eastern edge. This was Maliniam, the Dawn Star, also white, and slightly fainter than the Pole Star, but no less impressive when it appeared glimmering over the shoulder of the great mountain range that was said to have the shape of a sleeping lion. If the White Bear was the watchfire of the gods, guiding travelers on their paths, then Maliniam was the unclouded single eye of Jarn, always commanding the earth below but never responsive to its pleas. Indeed, many called the dawn star "Jarn's Eye."

The stars drifted across the night sky, and their silent music calmed the hearts of the Mongauli knights and their captives. All listened to the sound of the heavens and all were lulled by it. Even if it was merely the calm before a great storm, for the moment not a few of them forgot that they were beyond Janos' domain. They felt safe.

In the lady's pavilion, the lights were out, and all was silent.

Under the same sky, a restless shadow moved quietly through the darkness. It was tall and slender, and though it was both armed and armored, it was evidently the beneficiary of long training in the art of stealth. It managed to creep along noiselessly, keeping close to the hard rocky ground. It moved smoothly, supple and alert as a Danayn water snake.

The shadow had been tailing the Mongauli host since they packed up the lady-general's pavilion and set out towards the River Kes earlier that day. Always it maintained its distance, staying not too far and not too close, just remote enough to avoid the watchful eyes of the rear guard. Where there were boulders, it hid in their shadows. Where the land opened up into a wide plain, it crawled flat on the ground. When the sun was high in the sky, it stayed so far back that the knights were almost beyond its sight. When dusk came its pursuit became markedly easier.

There were a few close calls. Once, when the shadow came too near, Captain Astrias, a noble young man of Torus with an athletic frame and neatly trimmed black hair who was charged with leading the rear guard, saw something far behind the ranks catch and reflect the last rays of the setting sun. To his eyes it looked much like the metal buckle on a suit of armor. A scowl of suspicion came over the captain's swarthy visage, and he raised his horsewhip and muttered "What was that?" aloud, to no one in particular.

One of the men nearby peered out across the rocky waste. "I see nothing, sir."

The captain frowned thoughtfully. He was commanding the rear guard of a host led by the lady-general herself, and the responsibility lay heavy on his shoulders. He was prepared to ride back and see in person what, if anything, was back there, when a shout went up from the front of the line: "Bigeater!"

"Damn!" Astrias cursed and turned his horse to gallop back towards the main body of men. Soon all his attention was focused on keeping order among the ranks. The glimmering he had seen might have been a mirage or a trick of the eyes, and in any case, it was unimportant compared to the threat posed by the bigeater. If he remembered it at all, it was pushed out of his mind entirely when the angel hair came at nightfall.

So it was that the shadow had continued on unnoticed until

the day became quite dark, and the knights set up camp and lit their giant bonfire to keep the angel hair at bay.

The shadow was, of course, none other than the mercenary Istavan of Valachia. Clad as he was in the jet armor of a Mongauli black knight, he was emboldened by the fall of darkness, feeling free to come quite close to the knights' encampment. He was now weaving through the boulders towards the edge of camp, cursing under his breath.

"By the thirteen hag-daughters of Doal! Does this accursed place never rest? Damn the jelly freaks and damn this angel hair!" He paused to spit and think of what to curse about next. "The wispy stuff gave those Mongauli knights a turn, though, didn't it?" Istavan would not have admitted it, but he had been more than a little worried himself when the swirling white mist had grown thicker than any angel hair he'd ever seen before.

"Then again," the mercenary mused, "all this will make a fine old tale to tell my grandchildren, when I'm an old man, sitting on the stone step outside my house by the sea."

Istavan was pleased to observe that many of the knights, wearied by the run-in with the angel hair and the battle with the bigeater, were now taking turns sleeping. The watch was light. Scrambling over a small outcropping, he saw what he was looking for: the commander's pavilion, where the knight in the shining white armor whom he'd seen earlier was probably quartered. "Just who was that?" Istavan mused under his breath. "It might have been a trick of the sun's glare, but I'd swear by the light of Jarn's Eye that his hair was made of pure gold. A young leader, that one."

Istavan thought back through the officers that he knew were among the ranks of the white knights. There was Count Vlon, and Baron Lindrot, but they were too old to be the knight in white. Then there was Raias, Allion, Rentz...

Hmm...maybe it was Sir Allion? That would make sense, but still...Doal-spit!

Istavan had been weaving his way towards the pavilion to get a closer look at things when he heard low voices talking, men chatting on patrol, far too close for comfort. In his surprise, the mercenary had almost sworn out loud. Swiftly, he dropped into the safety of the nearest deep shadow and held his breath.

"A bit harsh, don' ye think? A captive's a captive, I know, but they're only children!"

The answer came in the rough rasp of an older knight with a heavy accent. "'Tis not for us to question th' general's plans."

"I know they're to be put on the rack once we return, but still—"

"Just think they've been put on th' rack ahead of schedule, then, and stop yer worrying. I know I've had a few regrets meself, that girl there's a prize. Still a bairn to be sure, but a passing lovely 'un. Ye can tell by her skin she's royalty. I'd hate to see those pretty hands and legs on the wheel-table."

"Shh!"

With a rustle, someone opened the entrance flap to the general's pavilion. The sounds of a conversation spilled out into the night.

"Rest well, General." The voice belonged to a heavy-set man dimly visible as he paused at the opening. But the voice that answered him was young—extremely so—and, Istavan thought, rather severe.

"Tell your men to be prepared to march at first daylight. The horse we sent ahead should have arrived at the fortification by now. We can expect a welcome force to come meet us halfway to the river. And make sure the watch is kept tonight. Ah, and tell Lindrot…"

"Yes?"

"Tell Lindrot to keep a close eye on the captives. I don't want them biting off their tongues or any such foolishness."

"As you command."

"Astrias!"

Istavan heard a grunted reply from further inside the tent.

"Kayn will bring up the rear tomorrow. You'll be riding in the middle. I know it can get tiring back there."

"It's really no…Hmph, I understand, General." The one who must be Astrias sounded vexed at the command, but spoke no further. The pavilion entrance flap was lowered.

Istavan crept closer. Perhaps he could look in through a slit in the side of the pavilion. He had to see who this general was who seemed so young, yet gave orders like a veteran commander. When he had peered down from atop the cliff earlier that day, he hadn't been able to see him clearly enough to satisfy his curiosity. There was something about that intensity, that almost arrogant lilt to the voice that filled him with an impulse to see his face.

The Crimson Mercenary stealthily advanced until he had reached the side of the pavilion. Then, finding a seam in the side where the panels of cloth had been tied together, he began slowly separating them. He could hear low voices inside the tent. He was about to peer in when—

"Aah!" Istavan yelped reflexively, then just as quickly slapped his hand over his mouth.

Something was on his other hand, a disgustingly bulbous, faintly luminescent grub-like thing. *Sandworm larva! It must have jumped on back there in those rocks and come along for the ride.* The nasty thing was on his gauntlet, trying to latch on and drain the blood from his hand. It had found the steel far too hard to penetrate and so it sat there, frustrated, waving its circular mouth in the air. The tiny red eye underneath its orifice was glaring at Istavan with the kind of malice toward life that only the spawn of Doal bear.

Yuck! Don't do this to me, Doal!

It was only a tiny sandworm, barely hatched, but still it looked so horrid as it flailed there and threatened him mindlessly with its goblet-shaped head that, almost by instinct, he knocked it off his hand and crushed it beneath his heel. Istavan was a hardened mercenary (Spellsword, no less) who generally feared little that could not kill him outright. But, truth be told, he had always felt a little unmanned by slugs and leeches and their ilk. Even through the thick sole of his boot, the sensation of the thing squishing made shivers run up his spine.

"Who goes there?"

Distracted by the larva, he had let a patrol get too close! Quickly he abandoned his espionage and bolted as fast as he could out of the range of the patrol's torches. Crouching low, he waited for the knights to decide that it had been an animal or a trick of the wind and lose interest. Eventually they did.

He had failed to catch a glimpse of the mysterious general, but the attempt had not been entirely fruitless. The very thing that had caused him to fail had suggested a new plan to the Crimson Mercenary. It might not have been the best plan—in fact, he could think of a number of reasons why he should not follow it—but he was running out of time. Pretty soon the first hoof-beats of Ruah Sungod's chariot would be ringing in the eastern sky.

"Doal!" Istavan shivered and cursed. "Damn the odds! I might as well try it. And if this goes as I hope it will, by the fifty-tad-wide moneybag of Igrek Fortunemaker, I'll claim a million-raan reward from those twins of Parros. I'm sure they've got that much ferreted away somewhere." So saying, Istavan headed out into the Nospherus desert on a reluctant search, trailing oaths as he went.

About a *twist* later, the eastern sky began to brighten, and the Mongauli soldiers were just starting to believe that they would make it through the night alive, when a scream went up from one edge of the camp.

"He-e-elp! Sandworm! Sandworm after me!"

"Where? Where?"

"Sandworm!"

In moments, the camp became as frantic as a broken bee-hive. An impossibly large, leathery, segmented sandworm was plowing through the knights' defenses, heedless of the flames, snatching up unlucky men in its path and draining them of life. Military discipline dissolved into chaos.

Of the foul denizens of Nospherus, sandworms were among the most fearsome. Gigantic, ravening life-forms, mindless and primitive, they felt no pain, and they would keep moving and attacking even if cut in two. Only by slicing them into tiny pieces or by destroying their primordial brains could they be stopped.

"Help!"

"Guard the pavilion!"

The air was rent by screams and the futile shouting of orders. The horses brayed and reared, and most of the knights were running in confusion.

A terrified captain came running into the pavilion. "My Lady! You are in danger! We must leave!"

Amnelis shook her head. "Send crossbowmen to the front! I'll take command!"

The unattended watchfire had begun to smolder. In the gloom, no one noticed that a knight was approaching the captives, and no one saw that his armor was a curious mix of black and red.

A young knight still on guard protested when Istavan drew his sword and slashed away the captives' bonds.

Istavan grunted, "Captain's orders—we're to move them to safety!"

The knight, flustered, nodded briskly. "Need me to help?"

"No, have you a sword? Get after that sandworm! It just got another one of our brothers!"

Istavan had no need to pretend he was afraid. His voice was already trembling from the wild run back to camp with the sandworm he had lured out of its lair hot on his heels. The mercenary had used his own body as bait and had run like the wind itself, absolutely terrified.

"Doal-spit! By the two curving necks of Janos, this is the last time I help anyone!" he growled in a low voice as he cut away Guin's bonds and handed him a shortsword.

Without a word, Guin and the twins stood up, shreds of leather falling from their wrists. They were free. They ran to the far side of the camp, away from where the defenders and the sandworm were engaged in a pitched battle. Istavan and Guin caught two horses that were running loose in panicked circles. The steeds were already saddled and bridled, and the two warriors mounted, each seating one of the twins with him.

"East," said Guin.

"Hiyup!" the mercenary shouted, and gave his horse a swift kick.

His mount had already reached a mad gallop when an alarm call went up.

"The captives are escaping!"

Indeed they were racing out into the wildlands dawn.

Chapter Four

A VALLEY OF YIDOH

—— I ——

"The captives are escaping!"

Bent low over the backs of their horses, Istavan, Guin, and the twins heard the yells go up from the camp behind them. The shrill commands of Amnelis calling for the knights to give chase mingled with the screams and the clash of metal from the fight against the sandworm. The captains' voices were a desperate roar as they shouted themselves hoarse trying to keep order in the ranks.

The four escapees rode hard, putting distance between themselves and the camp. Soon they could no longer make out their enemies' words; the distant shouts became a faint, twisted sound like the far away baying of Garmr Hellhound robbed of a feast of souls.

Eastward they galloped, weaving through the boulders, the Nospherus dawn wind hissing through their horses' manes. The Dawn Star, Jarn's Eye, grew dimmer as the sun threatened to pierce the sky above the crooked lumps of the Kanan mountains. Ahead of the four companions stretched open country—and freedom.

"Hyup! Hyaah!" Istavan spurred his horse, goading it on to

greater speed. He thought he could hear the shouts of pursuers beginning to ride on their trail, and he expected arrows or crossbow shot to follow soon after. The back of his neck tingled, as if a long hand might reach out from behind and yank him back at any moment.

By comparison, Guin seemed calm as he rode with the boy Remus clinging tightly to his waist. He gave a slight pull on the reins and rode close alongside Istavan.

"Slow down! Push your horse too hard and she'll tire."

Istavan, riding with Rinda in the saddle in front of him, turned to look over his shoulder.

The Mongauli camp was disappearing into the morning glare behind them, becoming a faint mirage, no more than a patch of moss on the ground between the white- and ash-colored rocks. He noted that no menacing cloud from the hooves of pursuers was yet rising and allowed himself a sigh of relief and then a flood of outrageous oaths.

"By the fire-breathing black swine of Doal, the muck that cakes its buttocks, and its keeper who's filthier still! That's the last time I do *anything* like that! I swear it, the last—"

Istavan stopped, not because he was through swearing, but because he heard someone softly speak his name. It was Rinda, her voice choked with emotion, her face twisting as she tried to smile through her tears.

"Th-Thank you, Istavan," she said. "And...and please forgive me. I thought you were gone. I thought y-you were off sleeping somewhere. But you w-were being chased by that sandworm, and...forgive me! Strike me down for doubting you,

Istavan."

"Ha," the mercenary replied, in the foulest of moods, "if I strike you, will you give me gold? Because I don't need your thanks, o most annoying of Parros pearls. I'm a fool to have done what I did. By the tattered turban of Jarn, I am a fool! I ignored the first rule of the mercenary, which is: *never* do anything 'less you're paid. And the second rule: no attachments. So kill me before you thank me, your highness, and give me gold before that!"

Riding alongside, Guin listened to Istavan's rant in silence. He said not a word, and his leopard mask prevented him from even smiling. But there was a twinkle deep in his yellow eyes that said he was greatly amused. For Guin could see that Istavan Spellsword, though he showed no outward sign of it, blushed on the inside as pink as any rose.

Rinda, still on the edge of girlhood, did not know enough of men to understand Istavan's outburst.

"Why of all the uncouth...Istavan of Valachia, I'll not have you speaking such oaths around me! I am a lady, you know!" the princess exclaimed, sliding forward in the saddle and trying to ride with as much dignity as she could muster. "If my thanks are of such little worth to you, then don't accept them. In fact, I take them back! And don't you whine about working for free. We may not have anything now, but if Parros should ever rise again, you'll be repaid tenfold for your services. Does that satisfy you?"

"Ha, you promise you'll pay?" Istavan grunted, looking unimpressed. "The Crimson Mercenary doesn't work for a pittance, I'll have you know."

"Oh yes? How much is your fee?"

"One million raan."

"Far more than you're worth!" Rinda sneered, flushed with fury. "You would take advantage of us!"

"Oh, I'd accept rank instead, if you find my price too dear. Make me a noble!"

"You, a noble? Never!"

"Is that any way to speak to the man who just saved the prophet Rinda Farseer and her crown prince brother from painful torture and a public execution at the hands of their Gohran enemies?"

Rinda's face had been coolly indifferent until Istavan mentioned torture and execution. Now she frowned uncertainly, and said, "Very well. I, Rinda Farseer, promise that when Parros stands again, you will be appointed a captain in the Holy Knights of the Crystal Palace."

"Be careful what you promise, little princess. If your plans for Parros turn out to be more than just a fairytale, you're stuck with me!" Istavan laughed. Yet he knew that by accepting such a promise even in jest, he was betting on the resurrection of Parros. But then, it occurred to him, perhaps he already had.

Oblivious to the mercenary's profession of faith, Rinda simply assured, "The royal house of Parros is true to its word, and so am I, Istavan of Valachia. My word is my bond."

"Captain in the Holy Knights?"

"Yes."

"And you'll pay me for my services, too? Okay, not a million raan, perhaps, but a good amount?"

"Of course."

"Fine." Istavan licked his lips like a cat after drinking sweet milk. Then his eyes glittered as though he'd had an unwholesome thought of a kind he rather enjoyed.

"By the way," he added, "what we just agreed on was for saving you and your brother back there. Things are going to get worse from here on out, you know. Who knows how many months it'll take us to cross the wilds of Nospherus? And then we've got the ancient mountains of Kanan to deal with, and none of the legends they tell about those peaks are pretty.

"Say I get you through all that, and guard you until you arrive safely in Earlgos or Cheironia or wherever. Tell me: how will you reward me then?"

"Well, I…"

"Don't forget, what I just did was worth the post of captain in the Holy Knights of the Crystal Palace!" Istavan insisted, a sly grin on his face. "Let me know when you decide. And remember, whether you hire me or not, I'm a mercenary and I live by mercenary rules. If you hire me, I'll give my sword to you without further ado, and I'll serve you loyally until our contract expires or is annulled."

"I…I understand, but we are heirs to a throne without a country, or a treasury…" Rinda fell silent.

Istavan ran his tongue along his teeth and smiled. "I've got an idea! How about, for starters, making me the Duke of Crystal so I can sit right next to you in court? Sounds rather pleasant to me." Istavan had barely got the words out when he broke into side-splitting laughter, nearly falling from the saddle in his enthusiasm.

"My!" exclaimed Rinda, her face flushing red, "Do you even know what you're saying, Istavan of Valachia? The Duke of Crystal would not only be third in line for the throne, or my regent if I became queen, he'd be my husband!"

"Let's say I help you restore your kingdom. You still wouldn't want to marry me, princess?" Istavan cackled between peals of wild laughter. Suddenly, assuming a serious air, he said, "I don't think of myself as an unattractive man." Immediately he set to guffawing again, slapping his sides and rocking back and forth as the mare galloped on beneath them.

Rinda was almost too incensed to respond. "L-Let me off this instant! Stop this horse! I will not sit here and allow such a foul-mouthed cretin to humiliate a princess of Parros! I'd rather take my chances with the sandworms! Stop this horse now!"

"Stop being so childish, the both of you," Guin demanded. Then he made a sound that was half a hearty belly laugh and half an animal howl.

"I see how it is," said Istavan, with what seemed like genuine displeasure. "Yes, of course the very thought of me becoming your husband does shame to the royal house of Parros. After all, I am but the son of a poor fisherman of Valachia. I'm a nobody, born with mud between my toes, and a corpse thief on the battlefields since the age of four. Don't think I don't know how the world works! So I apologize for shaming you, princess, but do remember this: I was born with a gem in my hand, and the moment I popped out, the village fortune-teller declared that I would one day be king, and that my kingdom would be given me by the Shining Lady!"

"You never told us that part," Rinda said, frowning.

"I'm telling you now! And the morning I become king, you'll remember the honor I offered you, and how you threw it in my face!"

"I never—"

"Stop it! Both of you," Guin ordered, seeing that, left to their own devices, the two would keep arguing until one of them fell off the horse. "She's still a child, Istavan," he said, but no doubt he thought the same was true of the merceneary. Rinda stared out over the wildlands, anger smoldering in her eyes.

Dawn had broken. Another hot day was beginning in the no man's land. The sky was a hazy violet-blue, stretching over an expanse of ashen, lichen-streaked rocks. The only things that moved were thin wisps of angel hair drifting from an unknown source, dancing on the wind before they melted back into nothingness.

Seeing that barren landscape reminded Rinda of something, and forgetting her anger for a moment, she peered over her shoulder at Istavan again.

"Suni! What happened to Suni? You...you didn't eat her?!"

"Please," growled Istavan, still glowering. "That skinny, smelly monkey? She took off for the hills as soon as she saw that you'd be captured. Aye, bounding off over the rocks she went, looking as happy as could be. Ingrate monkey! Well, can't say I ever expected more from that one."

"Suni...ran away?" said Rinda, shocked. She'd grown fonder than she'd realized of the furry little friend she'd met in the tiny room at the top of the tower in Stafolos Keep. More than anything, it had been a comfort to know that, no matter what trouble Jarn set upon them, she would have Suni by her side and they would face it together.

Rinda fell silent and turned away from Istavan, giving herself over to the swaying rhythm of the horse as it picked through the rocky terrain. Her violet eyes were filled with distrust and defiance, and her brows were marked with sadness. She said nothing more as they rode on through the endless Nospherus wildlands, the hoof beats of their horses echoing off the desolate rocks.

They had ridden steadily in silence for a while when Guin called out to the others in a low voice. "Look."

They twisted in their saddles as he pointed and looked back along the way they had come. A small cloud of dust was rising in the west.

"They're catching up," Istavan cursed under his breath.

Guin nodded.

"I was wondering when they'd catch up. We had a good lead, but even so, things were going too well."

As they watched, the dust cloud grew gradually larger. They could feel their horses beginning to tire; even though the twins were light, the steeds could clearly not continue for much longer carrying a double load. Their speed had been slowly decreasing, and while Istavan and Rinda were arguing, their pursuers, fueled by rage, had been steadily gaining on them.

For a short while, no one spoke. Finally Istavan turned to the leopard-man. "So, Guin, what do you think we should do?" he asked.

Guin hunched his shoulders. "You have any ideas?"

"Yeah, hide! If we can't fight and we can't run, it's our only choice!"

"Hide..." Guin echoed. He seemed to be considering the idea. "How long do you think we could hold out?"

"We can't do that!" Remus exclaimed, breaking in. "They'll keep searching until they find us, and we have neither food nor water, but they do! All they have to do is wait!"

"No one asked your opinion, kid," said Istavan with a scowl. He turned back to Guin. "Got a better idea, leopard-head?"

"No, that I do not..." replied the huge warrior, a resigned tone in his voice.

"Then what?"

"You said we cannot run or fight, but I disagree."

"What, you would stand against them?" Istavan laughed incredulously. "Hah! By Ruah's fiery sword, you're a fool!" The mercenary spat and twisted again in his saddle, squinting, trying to get a better look at the chase party.

"Can you see them? Are they more than a squad, Crimson Mercenary?" Guin demanded.

"Of course I can see them...these eyes of mine can pick out a balto bird atop a tree at one thousand tads! I'd say there's a full troop back there...red knights, with two of the white at their head."

Guin seemed to be weighing their chances.

"Hmm...add two more squads to that," the mercenary reported.

"Not good," said Guin slowly. "But we will do what we can. Istavan, I don't suppose you know the lay of this land?"

"Not a bit," Istavan admitted. "And I dare say I like it that way."

"To our east—those black lumps are the Kanan mountains, of which the ancient tales are told."

"That much I know."

"We won't be able to make it to the mountains, but the Raku tribe's village, of which Suni spoke, should not be far. She told me that her village lies 'where the Dog's Head is your finger,'" said Guin.

"What in Doal's name is that supposed to mean?"

"Do you see the mountain farthest to the left? That is the sacred peak of Pherus, the highest in the Kanan range. Seen from this side, it is said to look like the head of a dog, and thus its alias, Dog's Head Mountain."

Istavan cast Guin a dubious look.

"We can only see half of the head from here, but..." Guin stretched his hand out toward the mountain and raised one finger. "Close one eye, and look at your finger. Now, if you ride to where the height of that finger matches the height of the Dog's Head, the village of the Raku will not be far."

Guin turned and gauged the distance between them and their pursuers, who were now so close that individual knights could be seen galloping ahead of the rising cloud of dust.

"The three of you won't be able to go too fast on one horse, but go as far as you can," he instructed.

"Huh?" Istavan grunted, a puzzled look on his face. Then his dark oval eyes went round. "Hey, leopard-head!"

"And I've lost my sword. I'll need to borrow yours, mercenary."

"W-Wait," Istavan stammered.

"What are you going to do, Guin?!" shouted Rinda.

"Do not worry. I know many ways of dealing with men." Guin laughed a hard laugh. "Children! What our Crimson Mercenary has said might indeed be true. Nospherus may be my homeland. I'm starting to realize that I know this place, its creatures, and its land as though I have always lived here."

"Guin! I can't let you do this! It's not our right to demand this sacrifice of—"

"You have demanded nothing! I do what I will!" Guin interrupted. He lifted Remus from the horse and, prying away the hands that clung to his waist, tossed the little prince through the air towards Istavan. Istavan wheeled his horse and caught Remus just in time. He hefted the boy onto the rump of his mount.

"Guin! No!" screamed the twins in unison.

Ignoring them, Guin stretched out his hand toward the mercenary. Istavan unbuckled the sword at his waist and threw it to him, still sheathed in its scabbard. The leopard warrior snatched it out of the air and held it aloft in his powerful hand.

"Guin!" protested Istavan.

"Do not worry. See you in Suni's village." Then Guin

laughed again, a fearless howl that startled the twins.

The Mongauli search party was emerging from the dust cloud now, so close that they were plain to see. The clanging of their armor could be heard over the heavy drum of hoof beats. Their threats and cries to halt carried on the wind and could be made out: "Hey...Over there...Hold...."

"Go! Now!" barked Guin, waving his sheathed sword through the air. "We'll meet in the Raku village!"

"Right, the village of the Raku! Where the Dog's Head is a finger tall!" shouted Istavan, abruptly digging his heels into the side of his horse. Rinda clutched his leg, trying to stop him.

"No! We can't leave Guin! Please!"

"Get off me, kid! We're off!"

Guin swept past on his horse and gave Istavan's mount a smack on the rump with his scabbard. The exhausted mare, startled by the sudden abuse, found the last of her strength and set off at a gallop. "It shouldn't be more than three tads from here! I will see you soon!" Guin yelled. Then he wheeled around and charged towards the knights without looking back.

"Halt, fugitives!"

"Halt or we shoot!"

The shouts of the pursuers buzzed around Guin like stone shot from a hundred crossbows. Guin, standing tall in the saddle, gripped his horse's reins with one hand and, holding the scabbard between his teeth, used his other to draw the sword.

"Stay where you are, leopard-freak!"

"Do not resist, and we will spare your life!"

Guin paid no more attention to the cries of the knights than he did to the whine of the wind or the softly falling angel hair. Quickly he surveyed his surroundings. Had there been a sand-worm nest nearby, or even a pack of bigeaters, his task would have been relatively easy; he could have provoked them into attacking the cavalry, making unwitting allies out of the Doalspawn. But when such tactics were unavailable, there was always the way of the sword. Guin sized up the knights—two hundred strong, he could see—riding toward him in tight formation, and he growled low.

"Guin!" came a voice from behind him, and the sound of hooves.

"Fools! Why have you come back?" the leopard-man howled. His eyes burned with genuine fury.

"Guin, it's no good," shouted Istavan, his voice quaking. "Look!" He pointed eastward, the direction in which they had thought to flee. The children were clutching onto his saddle, their lips pale with fright as they looked desperately at the leopard-man.

Guin narrowed his eyes, and the burning wrath that had shone there a moment before vanished in comprehension. On the plains to the east, where they had hoped to find haven from the Mongauli, he could see another cloud of dust signaling the rapid approach of another search party.

"A pincer attack...with us in the middle," breathed Istavan.

A shrill, pained sound came from Guin's clenched jaws.

It almost sounded like a growl of despair.

—— 2 ——

Rapidly the two dust clouds closed in on the four companions, like dread jaws shutting on hapless prey.

"Guin. We're finished," said Rinda in a small voice. Her eyes were brimming with tears. "We'll be taken back, and there will be no escaping this time. I can only hope that those devils of Torus will have the sense of honor to give us a dignified death. Neither Remus nor I will ever forget, Guin, how you chose to sacrifice yourself for us, how you fought for our lost kingdom! Not until our last breath. And, Istavan—" Rinda turned to the mercenary. Her violet gaze met Istavan's eyes of obsidian, which were now opened wide in astonishment. "Thank you. Thank you for rescuing us from the encampment. I am sad that we won't be paying you for your troubles. You...You would have looked dashing in the fur-rimmed cloak of the Holy Knights! Tell them what you have to, do what you have to! You, at least *you*, must survive! You alone stand a chance!"

Istavan blinked. He had not expected such a heartfelt outburst. He was mumbling something about not having done half of what he should have done when Guin interrupted with a commanding growl.

"Don't give up hope! Children of Parros, I have told you
before: you must fight until the very end. Even if you do not lift
a sword, you must fight!"

"B-But—" Remus said.

"Wait!" Istavan cut him off. The mercenary's voice was filled
with a strange tension. "Wait, something's strange about that
other dust cloud!"

"What?!" This was Rinda.

"They...It's..."

What happened next convinced the twins that the mercenary from Valachia, driven to the depths of despair, had lost his
mind. For the slumped Crimson Mercenary suddenly sat
straight up and began to laugh so hard that they feared he would
break in half.

"Istavan!" yelled Rinda. Guin's eyes narrowed.

"Ah, ah hah hah! I see it now! What timing!" shouted the
mercenary breathlessly, pounding the saddle with his fists and
howling with a delight made all the more sweet for having
emerged from the blackest pits of despair.

"Ho!" Guin let out suddenly, with as much mad energy as
Istavan.

"Guin, what—" began Rinda.

"Suni!" Guin hollered with ferocious joy. "Ride, Istavan!
Ride east, and keep your bodies low to the horse. Make haste, or
we'll get in the range of the knights' pellet-crossbows. Make
haste!"

"Hiyup!" shouted Istavan, kicking the sides of his poor
horse again. "Hang on, kids!"

"What *about* Suni? What's going on?" exclaimed Rinda, still not seeing.

Istavan had turned their horse around once again. They rode towards the oncoming cloud of dust in the east. "Suni's brought the Sem to save us!" he shouted to the twins. "The little monkey's come to our rescue, and none too soon! We were in the bigeater's mouth, we were!"

"Suni!" Rinda cried, and then she could say no more, for her voice was choked with sobs.

The wildling warriors approaching across the desert plain were now clearly visible to Rinda as she peered forward over the horse's neck, and to Remus as he bent in the saddle behind Istavan. The Sem force had seemed farther away than it actually was; they were only half as high as their Gohran counterparts and ran on foot. Istavan urged the stumbling horse on toward them, knowing that it galloped on the very edge of exhaustion.

The approaching Sem war party consisted of diminutive but ferocious soldiers. Red war paint brightened their faces, and on their backs they bore leather quivers and short bows strung with vines. Their quivers bristled with poison arrows, and their bodies were adorned with strange animal skins and the feathers of exotic birds.

And there, at the front of the pack, a small, familiar shape ran with bounding steps, so fast she was almost tumbling towards them.

"Suni!" Rinda called out, jumping off the horse as they drew near the Sem. She landed awkwardly, falling to her knees, but was quickly up and running. She paid no heed to the sand that dragged at her ankles and the jagged rocks over which she stumbled.

"Riiinda!" Suni answered Rinda's call. Her little simian face bore a look of utter devotion, and tears of joy streamed from her eyes.

"Suni!" Neither of the two girls even noticed the bow shots from the Mongauli soldiers peppering the sand around them as they embraced. Both of them were sobbing convulsively and calling each other's names so often that they could scarcely spare the breath to say anything else. They were of different races and different upbringings, and neither knew a word of the other's tongue. But they discovered, there on the Nospherus sands, how deep their friendship was, two girls who looked as unlike each other as one could imagine two girls looking.

"Suni! My dear little Suni! You were a true friend!" Tears streaming down her face, the princess thanked the Sem.

"Alura, alufeh, emiiru, allu, elaatu!" chattered Suni excitedly, hopping with pride as she pointed at the small army behind her. Istavan sprang from the saddle and came running toward them with Remus at his side. Their horse, meanwhile, collapsed upon the sand, foam flecking its lips as it strained to breathe.

"One, two, three...I'd say there's about three hundred of them, plus me and Guin, against two hundred Mongauli knights. I'd say our chances are bloody good now," beamed Istavan, as though the Sem had arrived through some effort of his own.

"Noble lady!"

Rinda stood up, startled, to see who had called out to her.

Suni stepped away from Rinda and smiled, pointing at one of her fellow Sem. It was clear at a glance that this Sem was of high rank, a leader among his kind. He spoke Rinda's language falteringly but with only a trace of an accent.

"As thanks for saving a daughter of our tribe, we offer our humble assistance in your fight, and we request that you join us in our village."

"I, I don't know what to say—"

"I am Loto, chieftain of the Raku tribe. I see you are weary. Please, take refuge behind our ranks."

Rinda wondered where the little chieftain had learned to speak the language of the Middle Country so politely. She found herself naturally falling to one knee in the greeting of the high court in Parros, taking his furry hand in her own. "I am a prophet of Parros, the princess Rinda. This is my brother, Remus, the sole legitimate heir to the throne. Istavan of Valachia is our friend."

"This is no time to be playing palace with monkeys!" yelled Istavan, unable to contain himself. "Look! By the double-edged sword of Cirenos, leopard-head is taking on all two hundred of those Mongauli knights by himself!"

Rinda remembered where she was and spun around. Behind them, a furious battle was underway. Rinda had been too preoccupied with her reunion with Suni to notice that Guin had not accompanied them on their flight into the safety of the Sem ranks. While she had been weeping with joy, Guin had surged toward the enemy, howling an animal challenge, sword held high in his hand—a cavalry attack of one warrior against two hundred knights.

A shout of surprise went up from the knights as the battle was joined.

"Hold—you'll hit our own men!"

The Mongauli host was uncertain of how to deal with the terrible lone rider who plunged into their midst like an awl into corkwood. Fearing his fiery spirit, they gave way before him. At last the handsome Captain Astrias waved his red commander's flag and drew the knights back into formation, barring Guin's path and closing in to counterattack.

Guin's longsword hewed through the foes who surrounded him, cutting down horses and spilling shocked riders onto the unyielding ground.

"Do not use your crossbows! I want him taken alive!" yelled Astrias. He spurred his horse and headed towards where Guin was so skillfully overthrowing the red knights. It irritated the captain that he could not fight to the death against this opponent; the archduke's daughter had issued strict orders to bring back the leopard-man alive. If Saim and Feldrik, the white knights sent to oversee his mission, had not been there, he would have simply ordered the leopard-man killed and made up some tale later to please the general.

"Fight! Fight! He is only one!" Astrias shouted, urging his wary knights onward. But while it was true that Guin battled alone, he fought with the strength of ten. Red blood flowed down red armor and a great war cry went up from the leopard jaws. It was as though the legendary beast-god Cirenos was among them, singing his song of screams and dancing his blood dance, engulfing their very souls. Horses fell, their legs chopped out from underneath them, and even the bravest of the red knights hesitated, none wanting to be the next to challenge this fearsome champion.

The obvious reluctance of his men infuriated Astrias all the more. "You! How dare you retreat? We are knights, and he is one against us all! Surround him and bring him down!"

But before he was finished yelling, another foe appeared, on foot. Though his faceplate was lowered, this one in jet black armor was clearly a man.

"I'll watch your back!" the new arrival yelled to Guin. Then he pulled one of the red knights off his horse and jabbed him with a quick, lethal thrust of his shortsword. Fast as a panther, he snatched up the fallen knight's sword, jumped astride the horse, and fought his way towards the leopard-headed warrior.

"Guin! Are you all right?" the man asked above the fray.

"I was wondering where you were!"

The two warriors weaved their horses expertly through what had seemed a solid wall of knights, slashing and cutting until their mounts stood rump to rump.

"Guin! First time we fight together!"

"Aye!"

Although they were hopelessly outnumbered, the two friends had managed to break up the formation of the knights around them. Now the riders were regrouping to face them, approaching, then withdrawing, like a living wave hesitant to die upon the rocky shore.

Then, like a storm-surge, the Sem poured over the nearest rise and charged into battle with their eerie cries.

"Aii, aii, aii!"

"Ii, iie!"

"Sem!"

"A Sem raiding party!"

Another tremor of fear went through the Mongauli ranks. Astrias saw his knights scatter, and lost all patience. He could hold back no longer. "For Mongaul!" he shouted at the top of his lungs, and giving his tawny steed a sharp crack of the whip he charged straight into battle. So swiftly did he go that Saim and Feldrik, waiting beside him, could not react quickly enough to call out to him to stop.

The two forces clashed with the might of two giant sand-worms defending their territory to the death. But once they clashed, the Sem scattered amongst the knights so that the struggle resembled more that of a giant red sandworm that blunders into a nest of desert ants and is quickly buried under the swarm.

The Sem warriors ran between the horses, firing poison-tipped arrows with precision into the chinks in the Mongauli's armor—at their throats and armpits and through the eye slits in their faceplates. Stricken knights, clawing at their wounds, yelped and fell from their horses. As soon as they crashed onto the ground, Sem swarmed on top of them and finished them off with knife and ax.

The carnage was not one-sided, however; the blades of Astrias and his knights sent many a Sem head flying. The horsemen delivered sweeping cuts from above, sometimes slashing through two Sem at once. But the ape-men were cunning, and they had developed tactics for dealing with men on horseback. One of the tribesmen would run close to a mounted warrior and plant his feet, while another sprang atop the first one's shoulders. Then a third and a fourth ran up the pole created by the first two and leapt down upon a knight. Laden with their heavy plate armor, the knights were helpless against tiny Sem warriors who slipped past their swords and shields to cling to their breastplates. The knights' cumbersome gauntlets made it difficult for them to fight at close range as the wildings, like implacable fleas, went to work with their knives, stabbing furiously at the chinks between armor plates until they drew blood.

Seen from Ruah's bright chariot, now high in the sky, the battle must have looked like an undulating stain of rusty red blood on the white and tan of the Nospherus desert. The battle cries of the knights and the eerie shrieks of the Sem mingled and echoed through the desolate field of boulders.

"Allu, alurah! Alphetto!"

"Yii yii yii!"

"For Mongaul! For Mongaul!"

"Slaughter them!"

The Sem surged against the ranks of red knights, and the red knights pushed back. Meanwhile, the two white knights had slipped towards the back of the Mongauli lines and were engaged in a whispered conversation.

"Feldrik, it seems our forces are outmatched!"

"Yes, both in number and—with those two captains of

theirs—in skill."

"Have you seen the leopard-man fight?!"

"How could I not? And that one in black—if I'm not mistaken, his armor is Gohran, though he bears no crest."

"A deserter, then? Or a traitor? This is grave indeed."

Feldrik's answer was cut short by a band of Sem who broke through the battle lines in front of them. The white knight yelled as he flailed with his whip, knocking down wildlings on either side. "Traitor or no, all this proves that Amnelis was right! The wildlings are allied with the orphans of Parros!"

"This could be a threat to Mongaul."

"Indeed!" Feldrik struck down another leaping Sem warrior. "We should ride back with speed to report this to the lady."

"What of Astrias?"

"The fate of Mongaul may depend on us! We cannot tarry!"

Feldrik and Saim locked eyes. Then both nodded and, wheeling their horses around, they galloped from the fray, directing their mounts back along the way they had come.

"Hyaah!"

A horsewhip cracked. In the midst of the blades and the blood, the only one who had noticed the flight of the two white knights was the leopard-headed warrior Guin. He roared. Several red knights moved to block his path, but he forced his way between them and rode hard to intercept the two fleeing knights.

"Mercenary! Don't let them go! They'll bring reinforcements!"

Istavan shouted his agreement and spurred his horse to follow after Guin. But the red knights fell into formation in front of him, blocking his way. Judging swiftly that he'd never make it in time, he stood in his saddle, and, in the Gohran manner, grasped the pommel of his sword in his palm and threw the weapon like a spear.

His aim was true. The broadsword caught Saim's white horse in the flank and sank in deep. The horse reared and Saim was thrown, crashing down headfirst on a rocky outcropping. Weaving past a few astonished knights, Istavan leapt from his horse and with his dirk dealt the finishing blow to the fallen white captain.

Guin was less successful in his pursuit. Other red knights had rushed to cross his path, and when he realized that he would never catch the fleeing rider, he grimly returned his attention to the battle at hand.

Feldrik galloped on, not even glancing back to see his comrade's end. Beating his horse with his whip stock to drive it ever faster, he quickly disappeared in a cloud of dust, heading towards the River Kes and the safety of Alvon Keep.

"You there!" a voice called out to Istavan just as he had spun around to remount. "You will face *me* now!"

Judging from his voice and bearing, the knight challenging Istavan was about the same age. In fact, the black hair and sparkling onyx eyes that could be seen despite the red helmet were not unlike Istavan's own. This other spurred his horse and rode up between the Crimson Mercenary and the fleeing Feldrik.

"Out of my way, dung-chucker!" spat Istavan, quickly

remounting.

"I am Astrias, captain of these men! Speak your name, you who wear our armor but fight beside the Sem! For your sake I hope you are merely a murderer, and not a traitor to Gohra!"

Astrias? The Red Lion of Gohra? Istavan frowned and stared at his opponent from under his lowered faceplate. Except for the color of the man's armor, it was almost like looking at his own reflection in a mirror. Astrias's hair and eyes were uncannily similar to Istavan's. If they wore the same armor and had their faceplates lowered, perhaps it would be impossible to tell them apart.

Yet there was something about his opponent—a noble dignity, blazing with the fire of a single-minded devotion to his country—that Istavan lacked. The mercenary watched his foe with a wry smile on his face, missing nothing. He decided that he did not like the Red Lion one bit.

"Astrias! Offer up your head!" Istavan shouted, forgetting entirely about the fleeing Feldrik. He made sure of his grip on his sword and charged across the sand towards his noble foe.

The young captain smiled grimly, raised his sword, and charged. They met halfway, their blades clashing in the air between them and sending blue sparks flying. Galloping past each other, they wheeled around and charged a second time, then a third.

By the third pass, the color began to drain from Istavan's face. He had taught himself how to survive on the battlefield; the trick was precisely to avoid direct confrontations with talented opponents like this one. He did not know how long he could hold out against a fighter like this who had no doubt been trained by the best palace instructors in the art of swordplay since he was a child. Even though the two were similar in strength, and seemed to be evenly matched in skill as well, the mercenary knew that in the end, formal training had a way of outclassing the rough and dirty fighting styles that were his own stock and trade.

Moreover, the former pirate's latest adventures were beginning to taking their toll. He was tired. His hand was sweaty, causing his sword to slip, and every blow he countered from Astrias's blade sent pain shooting up his arm into his shoulder.

"You'll need to do better than that to claim the head of the Lion of Alvon, knave!" Astrias shouted confidently. He had begun to sense that he had the upper hand in this match. He would not have been so confident had he bothered to look at the battle around him; the Sem had completely surrounded the red knights and were pushing in hard on those remnants too. But for all his successes on the battlefield, Astrias was only twenty, a young man more interested in sparring than in leading. In war, such youth was a disadvantage.

"State your name!" Astrias demanded of the mercenary. "My sword was not crafted for cutting down nameless foot soldiers who dream of knighthood, coward!"

If Istavan had learned anything in his years of freelance soldiering, it was that honor and dignity meant about as much as a sword with no blade. If you wanted to survive, you had to be realistic. So he called for help as loudly as he could: "GUIN! GUIN!"

The leopard-headed warrior had found himself in the midst of a wary circle of reluctant challengers. The number of knights who dared to come close enough to cross swords with him was dwindling rapidly. Hearing the call, he charged suddenly through a gap in the ring and quickly reached the mercenary, who gladly moved to put Guin between himself and the troop captain.

"Coward! That was supposed to be a duel!" Astrias roared, advancing nonetheless to meet the new challenger. This time, however, the tables were turned. Guin's strength, his skill with the blade, and his endurance were all far above those of the young captain. The second time they crossed swords, Astrias's blade went flying from his hand and he tumbled to the ground. In a flash, Guin was standing over him, the point of his broadsword tickling Astrias's unprotected neck.

"Kill me!" Astrias hissed through clenched teeth. His face was flushed with shame. "Kill me, now!"

Guin held his blade steady and stared down into the captain's youthful eyes.

"Demon breed! Bringer of hell to Gohra! Kill me now!" cried Astrias in frustration.

Behind him, Istavan was yelling for Guin to give the Lion of Gohra his wish.

But Guin heeded neither of them.

"I am Guin," he said to his defeated opponent. His voice was harsh and heavy from within the leopard mask. "I have a message for your lady general who fights and commands like a man. Leave the wildlings and the creatures of Nospherus alone, or I will stand against Mongaul for all eternity."

Then he withdrew his sword and bent to help Astrias to his feet. Stunned, the youth stared uncomprehendingly at the leopard-headed warrior. He could not believe, in the first place, that he had been so wholly defeated, and now he was being given his life and freedom. All through it he had suffered no more than a scratch, but, his eyes stinging with defeat, he rubbed his throat with his hand and stumbled towards his horse on unsteady legs.

At long last Astrias shouted the order to retreat, his voice hoarse and uncertain. The straggling knights heard his call and regrouped away from the wildlings. Of the two hundred knights that had joined the battle, only fifty remained.

—— 3 ——

It was a defeat that Astrias would remember until his dying day.

He had been born to a noble house, and had won victory after victory since first he rode onto the battlefield as a bold and ambitious lad of fifteen. He was a young lion of Gohra, a hero. He was next in line to inherit his father's title as count and his position as warden of Torus. Now the same Astrias had been outmatched by a rabble of barbarous savages—not just defeated but driven into headlong, ignoble retreat with eight score of his men slain by monkey-warriors only half their size.

Astrias's chiseled features, brooding in the shadows of his helm, were paler than the whitest parchment. He bit his lip and pounded his fists into his saddle time and again. To lose to the Sem! His pride as a warrior of Mongaul had been scarred for eternity.

The red knights of the First Troop of Alvon Keep were in full flight. And the Sem, who had it in their power to destroy them, had let them go at the urging of their ally Guin. From their chieftain on down, the Sem had desired to press the battle against the retreating knights, but they already revered the leopard-headed warrior as though he were the god of war come down to walk the earth. When he spoke against further slaughter, they held back.

"Why stop 'em, Guin?" Istavan demanded, looking displeased that the battle was over. "I'd like to teach Mongaul a lesson, myself. We could put the heads of arrogant young lords up on pikes in the sand. Soon enough they'll start to run away whenever they see us two shoulder to shoulder."

Guin shook his head gruffly.

"Why not?"

"Lord Astrias is from a good family and is a personal favorite of Archduke Vlad's. His father, Count Malks Astrias, is the archduke's right-hand man and the Lord Defender of Torus. Kill his son, and Mongauli retribution would be swift."

"Hmm, good point, leopard-head," Istavan admitted reluctantly, still disappointed at having missed the chance to deal more damage to Mongaul. "But wait! How come you know more about Torus than I do? I thought you'd lost your memory!" He stepped back and looked at the leopard-headed warrior suspiciously. Guin did not answer.

The sand was stained with the blood of the fallen. Picking his way among the Sem and human corpses, Loto, the high chieftain of the Raku, drew near to where Guin and Istavan stood. Rinda and Remus followed behind him. With his feather headdress and gray-streaked fur, Loto cut an imposing figure for one so small.

He came before Guin and Istavan and bowed deeply. When he looked up, his eyes were filled with admiration and amazement.

"Brave warriors!" The chieftain spoke in the most serious and measured tone his high Sem voice accorded him. "Alphetto God has sent you here, to this desert. The bows and arrows of the Raku are yours."

Five lesser chieftains lined up behind Loto. Now they all bowed and said as one: "Riyaad."

"They say in our language that you are the Leopard," Loto explained. "You are a child of Alphetto God."

"Hey, Guin, they're saying you're the son of a monkey-god," chortled Istavan.

Guin motioned for him to be quiet. "I am Guin," he said simply, matching the serious tone of the Sem chieftain. "I thank you for saving us."

Loto waived his hands. "No, no, Riyaad, it is I who must thank you for saving my grandchild."

"Suni?"

"Yes, my fourth grandchild. She had gone out to gather medicine herbs we needed for our desert rites, when the black demon came across the Kes and carried her away. The black demon peels our skin and drains our blood."

"You do not need to fear him any more. Guin took care of the demon of Stafolos Keep!" Rinda said proudly. She held Suni's hand tightly in her own.

Loto shook his head. "The black demon may be gone, but now the red demons cross in great numbers. Why are they so eager to assail us?"

"Your people were not at the attack on Stafolos?" asked

Guin.

Loto shook his head. "We Raku are peaceful. When the call
to attack came from the council, the high chieftains of the Karoi
and the Guro decided to go, but we Raku did not go. When
demons come, our way is to avoid them, to move away. We cannot stop the killing by becoming demons ourselves."

"Stafolos fell," Guin said, in a grim reverie of recollection.
"Many lives—both human and Sem—were lost."

"You and your noble companions are welcome among the
Raku, great warrior Riyaad. You may stay in our village as long as
you desire."

Istavan, looking somewhat dissatisfied, stepped up as if he
meant to speak. But all eyes were on Guin.

Addressing all the chieftains, Guin said: "You of the Raku
love peace, and avoid combat when it can be avoided. These are
great, no, these are wonderful things. And it is because you love
peace that I am troubled. During this battle, two white knights
broke away to head back toward the River Kes. We were able to
stop one, but the other escaped. If I am not mistaken, he is now
well across the river and has arrived at Alvon Keep. I fear he will
organize the knights there and launch yet another raid on your
land and people."

Loto turned and translated Guin's message for his lesser
chieftains. The worry in their eyes was clear.

"Is this the entire fighting force of the Raku?" asked Guin.

"Of course not!" replied Loto, rather proudly for one who
had proclaimed himself a pacifist. "The Raku are the largest
tribe among the Sem peoples, and our women fight alongside

our men. When there is war, only the old and the children guard the hearths. Our forces number two thousand strong." When he spoke the words for "two thousand," Loto reverted to the Sem tongue, using a phrase that Guin recognized as meaning "as many as the legs of two swallowworms."

Guin plunged deep into thought. Rinda, Suni, Remus, and Istavan stood quietly, awaiting his response, like children waiting for a parent's advice. Guin's stern, yellow eyes were inscrutable as his thoughts turned inward.

"Riyaad," said Loto, stepping forward. "I fear it is not wise for us to stay here any longer. Much blood has been spilled here. The bigeaters, sand leeches, desert ants, and worse will smell the feast, and they will come."

"Ahh…I had forgotten." Guin shook himself as though waking from a long sleep. "Then," he said, turning to Rinda, "We must leave."

"We will get to see Suni's village!"

"Yes, you will."

"But not you?" Rinda looked at the leopard-man, puzzled. "You are coming, too, aren't you?"

Guin spoke gently. "The white knight that escaped concerns me. Chieftain," he said, turning to Loto, who stood short but proud at the head of his retinue, "might I ask for fifty of your men? I need warriors to accompany me. I believe we would be wise to spy on the happenings at the River Kes. We will return to the village afterwards."

"As you wish, Riyaad Great Warrior," Loto answered, bowing his head. "Take whomever you will." He gestured toward his remaining troops.

"I ask also that you bring the children back to the village with you, Loto High Chieftain," Guin added, bowing in return.

"But Guin," Rinda protested, "You mustn't leave us!"

"I'll be back soon. I am only going to take a look," the leopard warrior said comfortingly, placing his strong hand gently on Rinda's slender shoulder.

Rinda shook her head, but could find no words to stop him. Her thoughts and fears whirled in a haze of fatigue.

"Eh, I, uh, I'm coming with *you*, right, Guin?" Istavan asked. "I don't talk the language these crazy monkeys use, and I swear some of those younger ones were looking at me and smacking their lips."

Guin hesitated, looking doubtful, but at last he nodded his assent. Then, turning to the Sem warriors gathered there, he called out in their language.

"Are there any of you who will go with me to spy upon the red demons?"

Fifty spirited young Sem stepped forward. None among them were wounded, and their fatigue from the battle had already passed. They stepped as lightly as if they had just awoken from a long nap on a bed of soft rushes back in their village.

"They are yours, Riyaad," proclaimed Loto.

Guin nodded. "I thank you. We will return to the village soon."

"Aye, and have a black pig roast, er…at least a sand leech roast waiting for us!" added Istavan, winking. Loto seemed shocked.

Guin and Istavan selected two new, untarnished blades from among the hundreds lying in the sand. Then they found two Mongauli horses that had lost their masters and mounted them after carefully examining the saddles, bridles and stirrups. The fifty Raku who were to join them on patrol went among those of their comrades who were returning to the village and gathered all the extra poison arrows that could be spared.

Just as the patrol party was making ready to leave, Rinda ran up to Guin and grabbed his horse's reins.

"Guin, take me with you!"

"I cannot."

"Please! I beg of you!"

"No, child. You have a true warrior's spirit—stronger than that of many men—but your body is still that of a little girl. A very weary little girl. You must go with Suni to the village of the Raku, and rest."

"Guin, I'm having a premonition, right now, a bad premonition. It isn't the worst of all possibilities, but it's something that could cause dire harm if it goes unheeded. Guin, please. Take me with you. My eyes can see into the mist that is the future. I can see around blind corners and warn you of danger! The sight is strong with me today, and I...I am afraid for you, because of what I see."

Guin thought deeply. Hope rose in Rinda then; but it sank again like a broken wave when at last he replied, "No. You must go to the village." He was gentle, but firm. "You said that what will come is not the worst? Then I will trust my strength, and my fortune, and this strange knowledge in my head that comes from I know not where. As long as I have these things, I will surely be able to cut through whatever misfortune might lie in wait. Do not fear, little princess. I will rejoin you soon."

"I understand," Rinda nodded glumly, but her eyes said she did not understand at all. Still she knew that Guin had made up his mind and that there was little she could do about it. After a moment she looked up at him again. "But you must let me tell you what I have seen so far. Guin, please listen carefully: Take care both as you go and as you return. Fear more that which you cannot see than that which you can. Fortune lies within misfortune, but you must beat down your own path if you wish to claim it."

"Is that all?" Guin asked.

"Yes, that is all."

"Sounds more like proverbs than prophecies," Istavan observed with a wry smile.

Guin clapped Rinda on the shoulder. "Let us both take care." The girl was not comforted, but she smiled, and gave Guin her blessings before walking back to where Suni stood.

It was time for the parting. Sitting tall on their heavy war horses, Guin and Istavan rode out ahead of the fifty Sem warriors, heading westward, while the twins and the remainder of the Sem turned eastward.

The Sem warriors who had been wounded in the battle were placed in the middle of Loto's ranks, where they could lean on their brothers' shoulders for support. The more seriously wounded were carried on makeshift stretchers crafted from bowstrings, but only those who seemed likely to recover completely were to be brought back. Any braves who had been so wounded as to be unable to fight again were abandoned among the dead. This was the law of the Nospherus wildlings. The desert was harsh and food was scarce. Those that could not fight or otherwise serve the tribe were left lying beside the bleached rocks under the harsh sun so that their families would not be burdened with the need to support them. There was no burial among the Sem. The denizens of Nospherus could be counted upon to clean up all traces of the dead and dying. The end would come quickly.

Rinda shivered. She had much love for Suni, and was glad to count the Raku tribe among the allies of Parros, but it was hard for her to accept their brutal customs. *Thank the stars that I was not born in the wildlands of Nospherus!*

When the two Sem forces began their march, the sun was high in the vault of the sky, and a dry, gusty wind had begun to blow the smell of blood from the battlefield in all directions. The moaning of the wounded and the whinnying of dying horses filled the landscape with the sounds of pain, while the eerie, inescapable angel hair drifted down to melt on the faces of living and dead alike, appearing and then vanishing like dimly remembered dreams or the first snowflakes of winter.

The warriors guarding the rear of each company of Sem were startled by a sudden commotion behind them. They waved their weapons and shouted their god's name. Guin and his party peered back at them and saw the sand under the battlefield swell and burst to reveal a horrid shape with flashing fangs.

"Riyolaat," muttered a Sem who stood near Guin, pointing

at the bigeater, which gorged its blood-red mouth on the corpses of the fallen Gohran knights, then vanished under the sand as quickly as it had appeared. Moments later, a pit opened up nearby, revealing the countless white tendrils of a mouth-of-the-desert reaching out from the sand to claim the bodies of three Sem. "Lalu," said the young Sem warrior.

Nospherus had begun its work of cleaning up the dead. By nightfall, all the men, wildlings, and horses would be gone. And by the time Ruah rose in the morning, the battlefield would have become indistinguishable from the vast reaches of that sea of white rocks and shifting sand. No one who passed would be able to guess that a battle had raged there only a day before.

Loto gave orders to march faster. It would not do to tarry. Once the cleaners of the Nospherus desert finished with the remains of the battle, they would turn to the only other source of food, the living.

The last thing Rinda saw when she looked back over her shoulder was Guin riding at the head of his tiny army, a proud half-beast god of war on the march to another victory. The leopard-man's force moved off into the desert and faded like a mirage.

Guin did not look back. Behind him the bigeater's jaws crunched bones and swallowed flesh in loud wet gulps, sounds that could make the hair on a man's body stand straight up. Yet Guin seemed indifferent to the gruesome noise.

"The knights are well ahead of us. We may not have time. Hurry."

He spurred his horse toward the west, toward the River Kes, and Alvon Keep, and the enemy general from whom he had escaped that very morning.

For a moment Istavan was doubtful that the Sem behind them would be able to keep up with the pace their leader set, but his worries were unfounded: all fifty of the diminutive warriors trotted steadily behind the two horses. The desert was their home, and their short legs navigated the shifting sands and sharp rocks with surprising agility.

After they had marched for about a *twist*, Guin's leopard mouth emitted a sudden low order to halt. The Sem ceased their movement more promptly than seemed possible and waited poised in silence.

"What is it?" asked Istavan. Guin pointed beyond a small rock outcropping that lay ahead of them.

"The remnants of Astrias's troop."

"They still lurking around? This is our chance, then. Let's take 'em!"

"Not so fast," growled Guin. "We are only fifty, separated from the rest. Do not forget that. Let us find a way through those rocks over there."

Istavan muttered under his breath, but then his face brightened and he chuckled. "Hey, Guin."

"What?"

"I just thought it funny that scarcely a few hours ago you and I were running scared from the Mongauli, just two swords against a host of knights, and our only treasure two tired orphans. Now we're hunting the Mongauli, and you're leading your own elite monkey squad like you were born for this."

"I was never scared."

"All right. But I bet that in your Randoch or Aurra, or wherever it was that you lived, you were some kind of a king, or a general at least. Aye, I'd bet it on the gemstone in my newborn hand that you were."

Guin did not respond.

Avoiding Astrias's knights, he led his party on a detour along a craggy ridge of rock. The Sem bounded lightly from boulder to boulder, and as they went they released vapors of an herbal concoction upon the wind to keep away the snakes and sand leeches and poured vials of another fluid to burn away patches of flesh-eating moss that lay across their path.

In a short while, they had reached a rise from which they could look down on the land to the west. From there, they could move along the ridge-top, keeping an eye on what was below them. The remnants of Astrias's company were progressing unsteadily towards Alvon. They were a straggling bunch much reduced from the force of proud red knights that had raced across the wildlands that morning in pursuit of Guin, Istavan and the children. Their horses were scarred, their armor broken, and the wounded cried out every time their mounts lurched or lost footing on the rocky ground.

"Just a little farther, and we'll reach the Kes. Just a little!" Astrias tirelessly shouted out, keeping his men moving despite their terrible fatigue. His throat was dry from the sand and the yelling, and there were times when the cries of the wounded threatened to drown out his words, but he rode back and forth along the line, keeping the weary knights in order and trying to encourage them as best he could. He was only twenty years of age, and his defeat at the hands of the wildling Sem was his first ever in the line of duty. It had dealt a fearsome blow to his pride. Though he was really the one who needed encouragement, he rode the line tirelessly, keeping a lookout for any foes that might be following them, any stragglers that might have drifted from his ranks. Now and then he would pause to give one of the badly wounded a drink from his own canteen. All hope of a personal victory was gone that day, but the youthful spirit of Gohra was strong within him, and it kept him moving when nothing else could.

Thankfully, none of the wildling Sem seemed to be giving chase. He doubted that his band would survive if they were to face another conflict now. Maybe the great sand leech god of the Sem, Alphetto himself, had favored the young noble, for he sent no bigeaters, sandworms, or any of the other dangerous denizens of his desert to hinder their progress. Astrias did not guess, nor were his eyes keen enough to see, that a leopard-headed warrior and a mercenary in the black armor of Gohra, mounted on Mongauli horses and followed by fifty Sem warriors, were looking down at his bedraggled troop from high above, their eyes glittering among the whitened rocks.

Some of the red knights, their scabbards long lost, were dragging their swords with drooping arms, banging them against the ubiquitous boulders with an irregular clanging that grated on the nerves of all who could still hear. The chorus of moans from the wounded and the faint melody of water sloshing in nearly dry canteens made for a ghastly accompaniment. The faces of the knights who had lost or raised their faceplates were dirty, rubbed raw by sand and speckled with dried blood.

Occasionally one of the wounded, hanging nearly lifeless over the neck of his horse, would simply cast away his heavy Gohran helm. When Astrias, constantly dreading the arrows of snipers, saw this happen, he would ride back and scoop the helm off the ground with the tip of his longbow, returning it to its owner with a gentle warning about the danger of an attack.

He had just returned another helm when a voice called out weakly behind him.

"C-Captain." It was Pollak, his lieutenant. Pollak seemed to be among those with at least some strength left, and one of a handful who were still bothering to watch for trouble.

"What is it?"

Astrias squinted and stared, but so much sand had caught in his eyes that even when he looked carefully in the direction Pollak indicated he could see nothing but a great hazy mist. Lifting his faceplate, Astrias took off one of his mail gauntlets and furiously rubbed at his eyes. They burned like fire, but they watered and he was able to focus.

"Captain," Pollak whispered again. Astrias thought he detected the faintest spark of joy in his lieutenant's voice.

"Halt...Halt!" Astrias licked his dry, broken lips and gave the order to stop. His heart was racing. He found it hard to believe what he was seeing. Surely it had to be a mirage. He blinked, but the vision remained.

"Pollak, go. Go see and report."

"Sir!" Pollak cried with a newfound strength, and urged his horse forward with a swift crack of the whip.

Astrias watched him ride, and he breathed in deeply. The shame and anger was draining away, leaving an almost mad joy in his heart and the sweet taste of hope on his lips. He could feel the energy flowing back into his limbs, and his face flushed with eagerness. When he saw Pollak disappear into a corner of the swimming mirage, he thumped his saddle with his fist.

"Leopard-headed monster, black-armored traitor, vile monkeys of Nospherus, hear me! Your luck has run dry…and the barbarian country's time has run out!"

—— 4 ——

Of course, the mirage-like image that Astrias and Pollak had seen as they rode across the plain was even clearer to the sharp eyes of Guin and Istavan high on a ridge above them. The two fugitive warriors first noticed it as a long, hazy line of rippling dust between them and the bluish sparkle of the Kes.

After a while, the wind shifted and the dust cleared, revealing its source.

"Down. Now!" Guin commanded, leaping from his horse even as he did. The Raku warriors did not need to be told twice. In a flash, they were down on their bellies amongst the rocks. Some had even nocked poison arrows in their bows and were searching warily for a target.

"Hold! Fire no arrows!" Guin hissed in the Sem tongue. "Stay low and do not move. If you wear anything that catches the light, put it under you!"

Istavan crawled behind the horses, which he had induced to lie down. After a few moments crouched in the open he realized that the black armor he wore would stand out like a signal upon the white ridge-cliff. Keeping close to the ground, he slithered over to Guin's side.

"Is that what I think it is?"

Guin merely nodded and growled deep in his throat.

Istavan swallowed and stared at the hair-raising sight away below them.

"By Ruah and his fiery host! Doal!"

Guin paid no attention to Istavan's curses. All eyes on the ridge-top were fixed on the the barren plains below, for what they saw was far more terrible than what any of them had expected. A vast army of Mongauli soldiers had crossed the river and set up camp in the wildlands, lining the eastern bank of the Kes so that not a square yard of earth was showing for at least a tad along the water.

Istavan's trained eye judged the host to be over ten thousand strong. The Marches sun glinted off the Gohrans' armor, their tall helms, and their weaponry, creating an unnatural shining lake that pushed against the desert like water brimming against a dam. "There's a company of the white in the middle. Those red knights on the right are probably the rest of the keep guard from Alvon. And the sea of blue on the left would be reinforcements from Tauride Castle. I wouldn't be surprised if Count Marus was out there leading the Eighth Blue Knights himself. And those black knights in the rear would be from Talos Keep."

Guin nodded, listening intently.

"Then again, they might be the first contingent of a full-fledged expedition from Torus. It's a possibility." Istavan spoke with apparent calm, but there was a slight tremor in his voice. "That's about ten to fifteen thousand men, I'd wager. Five thousand crossbowmen, three thousand infantry, and a good five thousand cavalry. You see the way they're lined up? That's a variation on the Mongauli quinticolor formation. They're missing one of the five colors, but they've still got enough to do their classic compass attack: one force from the north, one from the east, one from the south, and one from the west. D'you know why the Mongauli paint their knights like that, Guin? For one, it helps 'em not kill their own in battle, but more than that, it's so the general can see how each part of the force is faring and figure at a glance where to send reinforcements."

"They're just welcoming back Astrias's band," Guin noted. Then his voice grew thoughtful. "That warrior girl is their general, Istavan?"

"Aye. You see the white knights there? And their pennons? The flags flanking the one in the middle are the archduke's and Gohra's. The one in the middle's the banner of the archduke's daughter."

"And this girl intends to lead an army into the no-man's-land, and conquer its rocks and its dust, and its wildling tribes, peaceful or no." Guin spoke with a tone of such utter contempt that Amnelis would have been driven mad had she been present.

"That Mongauli general is one of the most famous warriors in the Middle Country. The archduke's only other child—his son, Mial—is a weakling, sick from birth, you see. Rumor has it she's planning on succeeding her father when he passes on. She's even got a fake moustache made just for the occasion!" Istavan chuckled. "Mongaul's got the same problem that Parros does!"

"What do you mean?"

"The hen is strong, and the rooster just shuffles around chirping with his birth-shell still stuck on his arse!" The mercenary held his hand over his mouth to hold in his sudden mirth.

Guin shook his head. "If you are speaking of Rinda and Remus, I think you've been misled by the boy's soft hair and softer personality. You're missing the dragon that sleeps inside, friend. I know that boy will—" Guin suddenly broke off as his keen eyes noticed a change in the forces arrayed below them.

He stated, with a sort of calm: "The army is moving."

It was a fantastic sight, awesome and uncanny, yet familiar, like an epic palace mural that has been seen for years but takes on a sudden power when one day its true meaning is finally understood. The Mongauli formation was an enormous three-petalled flower, red, blue, and black, surrounding a stamen of dazzling white.

Each petal that unfurled in the desert had a triangular shape made up of three tiers, the footmen outermost, the bowmen in the middle, and the horsemen innermost. The whole moved smoothly and without pause, as though it was not comprised of thousands of men but was a single giant organism. Its movements were guided by invisible threads that ran from the center of the formation; the white core controlled the flanks and the rear as though they were the limbs of a puppet and it the puppeteer. And though she could not be seen, there was no doubt that at the heart of the inner core, surrounded by dozens of flags and hundreds of loyal knights, was Amnelis.

"Blast it!" Istavan cursed abruptly. "How in Doal's name

did they get such an army here in such good shape in so little time! They would have to have been planning this for months!"

"Perhaps they were," Guin agreed. "Our arrival may have been the spark they needed, or perhaps we added oil to an already-burning fire. Either way, it seems that Mongaul made plans to conquer the Sem and the Lagon of Nospherus almost as soon as they worked out the taking of Parros. The Mongauli were concerned that, while they were reaching toward Parros, someone—perhaps one of the other archdukes, perhaps some Parros sympathizers—might attack Mongaul from behind where its forces would be thinnest."

Guin thought for a moment. "By joining with the Sem and routing Astrias's company, we gave credence to their worst fears—the orphans of Parros in league with the wildlings!"

Istavan nodded. "Aye. Then this is probably not the entire invasion force. I wouldn't be surprised to see another twenty to thirty thousand coming down from Torus. They're likely already on the highroad."

"Crimson Mercenary, we must take care not to lead them straight back to the Raku village. Against this host, an ill-prepared village of two thousand would not stand for a night. They'd be slaughtered in a *twist*, and us with them."

Guin turned to the warriors behind them and translated their conversation into the wildlings' tongue. The young Raku were worried. Their leader, whom they called "Siba," asked Guin in his high-pitched voice what he meant to do.

Guin told them in their tongue, "I intend that we return to your village with great stealth, and to make ready for battle. Or else the last days of Nospherus are at hand."

Istavan, picking up on the flow of the conversation, snorted into the dust. "You think a handful of monkeys can stand against this many veteran troops? If you do, then I'm touched, I really am touched!"

Guin looked directly at the mercenary and spoke calmly. "We know the enemy's plan, and they do not know that we are aware of them. This gives us the advantage. Moreover, they certainly do not know the precise location of the village. The Mongauli have not ventured more than a day's journey on horseback into Nospherus. Loto's village is hidden in a valley and it is hard to find. We may have five, even six days to prepare, Istavan."

"Why do you always know these things, leopard-head?" mumbled Istavan gloomily. "I suppose you know the exact location of this Sem village, to which you have never been?"

"Do not misunderstand," Guin explained. "I do not *know* all these things…nor am I certain about their village's location. It is only that I can see it dimly, and the lands around it, as though through a fog."

"Whatever you say, Riyaad-man." Istavan continued impatiently, "Look, I don't much care whether we run back and help them evacuate, or we run back and prepare for a doomed defense, but let's do something, for Doal's sake!"

Guin nodded and turned to give orders to the Sem warriors. The reconnaissance force had seen what it had come to see, and now all made swift preparations to leave. On the plain below, the Mongauli invasion force undulated with the strange grace of a giant amoeba as it slowly headed for the Nospherus interior. The tip of the left flank was now brushing the very cliff they stood on.

Guin spoke quietly to his young band. "We will keep among the rocks until we are out of their line of sight. Then we can go down to lower ground and move more quickly."

The small Sem nodded their assent and rose silently.

Shaking his head, Istavan, too, slowly began to rise from where he had gone to peer down one last time from the edge of the cliff. But as he did, his leather boot slipped on a patch of loose rock. He swayed and reached out hurriedly to grab Guin's outstretched hand, catching it in time to stop himself from falling. But he had knocked loose a cascade of sand, and it coursed down the steep grade, sending a handful of small rocks clattering down the cliff side.

With one hand the mercenary reached instinctively for the sliding rocks, as though he could stop them from falling. It was too late. Far below, a scout from the left wing of the Mongauli army heard the clattering of stones, on his armor no less, and looked up. He stood there for a long while, peering up the cliff wall, then turned and made signals to his fellow patrollers, gesturing also towards the main formation. Then Guin and Istavan, peering out from their perch atop the cliff, saw the man ride back to the main body of the army, where he made his report to his waiting lieutenant. A movement began backwards up the ranks. The message was being passed back to the center.

Whether it was the general who had given the order or not, the watchers could not tell, but suddenly the entire army came to a stop, as though pulled back by invisible tethers. Someone was taking the scout's report very seriously. Guin spotted captains bearing flags riding in towards the center of the army. An impromptu meeting must have been called.

"Now they know we're here," the leopard warrior said grimly. "The lady general means to send a squad or two out to look for us."

Istavan made it a point of not offering an awkward apology. All around him, the Raku stared with accusatory eyes.

"We leave," Guin announced. He ran to his horse and mounted swiftly. Istavan followed, eager to get going.

"We'll ride north. To go east now would be to lead them to the Raku village. Once we are sure they are misled, we will change our course to meet up with the others and warn them."

"Aii!" the Sem warriors bowed and exclaimed quietly, and the band began to move. Guin and Istavan rode swiftly northward along the ridge, weaving their way among the boulders, the little Sem running as fast as they could behind them to keep pace.

None of them could spare the time to look again at their enemies at the bottom of the cliff, where a small group of blue knights had broken off from the main host and was busily engaged in seeking a path up the steep, rocky incline.

"There!"

"Atop that mountain o' rock!"

For the third time in as many days, the leopard-headed warrior and the mercenary of Valachia heard the shouts of Gohran soldiers behind them in pursuit.

"Hyah!"

Guin and Istavan urged their steeds into a gallop. Now it was no longer merely their own lives, but the fate of the entire Raku village that hung on their survival. Even Guin kicked madly at his horse's flanks, and the fifty Sem who followed dashed on as fast as their swift feet would carry them, northward, toward where the Ashgarn Mountains towered, their peaks capped in eternal snow.

"Fly, Raku! Fly!"

"Riyaad! Aiii! Riyaad!"

The Sem moved as one over the dry Nospherus sands, which trembled and creaked under the pounding of their tiny feet. Glancing back, Istavan fancied he could hear them whispering in their strange tongue, pleading with the very sand they ran across: *O sand-God, you who have given us life, you who have raised us. Now we give you life: dance, o sand-God. Become a veil to shield us from the eyes of the demons...become blinding ash, a stealer of sight. Save the children of Nospherus from the fury of man and horse.*

The loud Mongaul-accented voices of the scouting party below them quickly turned into the whiz of bow shots, whirring through the air around them, ricocheting off rocks and streaking lines of blood where it grazed their speeding bodies. Puffs of dust leapt up from the ground ahead of them where stray shot sank in. Two or three Sem running at the very back were struck squarely and fell.

"Riyaad!"

Siba lifted up his bow and an arrow and knocked them together, signaling his desire to stand and fight.

"No, we must run!" shouted Guin, spurring his horse on faster. "Killing one or two won't make a difference."

"Gullah! Emiiru!"

Siba vented his rage, but he did not disobey the words of Guin Great Warrior. Once the Raku had sworn friendship, they were loyal to the end, and Siba was a Raku.

Though the Mongauli soldiers were mounted and the wildlings were on foot, the little barefooted Sem had the advantage in this deadly race. The rocky ridge proved inaccessible from below and so the soldiers, after firing several volleys at long range, were forced to make a long detour. Their horses were barded in iron plates, and the combined loads of barding, armored knights, and heavy war-tack weighed them down in the soft sand. The loose footing to the north of the ridge sucked at their hooves, and the fleet Sem sped ever further away. The soldiers cursed and lashed their mounts with their horsewhips, shooting their crossbows in frustration, but only two or three shots out of a hundred hit, and then finally even the rearmost Raku were far out of range.

At last the Mongauli, stymied by the rough terrain, were forced to cease their pursuit. They feared the wrath of their captain, but there was nothing to be done but gather up the bodies of the three Sem that their bow shot had felled and return with them to the main force. A strong wind had picked up, and it soon obscured the trail of footprints that was the Gohrans' only clue to the destination of the fifty or so Sem that had gotten away. The trail led north toward the towering Ashgarn Mountains.

Twilight was coming to the wildlands again. The unwelcoming wind blowing down from the Ashgarn range tossed clumps of angel hair into the faces of the invaders, and the knights from Alvon looked up with apprehension at the dimming sky and sighed, fearing the eerie Marches night.

After galloping steadily for at least three *twists*, Guin let his band slow its pace, giving the horses' weary legs much needed rest. They could no longer hear the voices of pursuers behind them, no longer did the bow shots fly. Coming gradually to a standstill, they caught their breath and called each other's names.

"We have lost three warriors, Riyaad," Siba reported.

I hope they are dead then, for their sake. Should they live, those gaudily painted demons will torture them horribly, Guin thought. But the words he spoke were stoic: "We were forced to take quite a detour. We will change course, now, and head east. Even if we have to risk traveling by night, we must warn the Raku of the Mongauli invasion as soon as possible. If we can be only a *shake* or even a *grain* faster, it may make all the difference."

"I understand, Riyaad. We are not tired. We will run through the night."

"No need to run. A fast march will suffice."

They changed course now and marched eastward. It came as a relief to them all to be able to put their backs toward the sun. Never dimmed by clouds, the Marches evening sun had become a huge and glowering orange disk on the horizon as it dipped down toward the Kes River valley. A giant evil eye: Doal was watching over his domain.

They followed a downward slope into a narrow ravine. The land rose on either side, growing steeper and steeper until the band marched between low cliffs.

"By Jarn," muttered Guin, wiping at the white silky strands that had begun to strike his face in increasing numbers. "By Jarn, there's a lot of angel hair here."

"Maybe we wandered into their town meeting," said Istavan gloomily. He had been in a foul mood since his blunder atop the cliff had alerted the Mongauli to their presence, precipitating the whole mad dash through the Nospherus wildlands.

Guin did not reply. He looked around and gave a low growl, almost too low to be heard.

The cliffs, left and right, continued to rise until they were walking in a gorge. Between the shadow-spawning walls of rock, they could see very little of their surroundings. Perhaps cued by the fading light, more and more angel hair were beginning to gather. The Sem seemed unfazed by the strange white substance that merely melted when it hit their faces, and they walked forward calmly wiping away the stuff with their furry hands. But Guin was becoming uncharacteristically anxious.

"Siba!" called out the leopard warrior in a harsh voice.

"Yes, Riyaad."

"You are sure this is the right path?"

"Yes, this leads to the village of the Raku."

"But look—the path becomes narrower and narrower!" Guin exclaimed, the worry clear in his voice. Istavan looked over at the leopard-headed warrior in shock. It was the first time he had ever known his strange companion to betray even a hint of fear.

Then they rounded a bend, and the entire party stopped, mouths agape. Before them stretched a scene out of a nightmare or the painting of a morbid artist gone mad.

The path fell away before them, spreading out into a large valley filled with a pale, bluish-white, eerily luminous lake!

Horror and disgust paralyzed their tongues, for the lake was no natural feature, but rather a vast pool of fearful life, a thronging mass of thousands—no, hundreds of thousands—of dripping, squirming, jelly creatures. They had stumbled upon a valleyful of yidoh.

The warriors' screams stuck in their mouths, and they felt the warmth of life drain from their limbs. They could not go forward, nor could they turn back. Numb with despair, they stood and watched.

And then they saw the seething pool undulate. The fell hive had noticed them.

And it was angry.